Predatory Kill

Kenneth Eade

Times Square Publishing
Beverly Hills, California

Copyright 2014 Kenneth Eade

Second Edition Copyright 2015 Kenneth Eade

ISBN: 1494988488

ISBN 13: 978-1494988487

OTHER BOOKS BY KENNETH EADE

Brent Marks Legal Thriller Series

A Patriot's Act

HOA Wire

Unreasonable Force

Killer.com

Absolute Intolerance

Involuntary Spy Espionage Series

An Involuntary Spy (Spy Thriller)

To Russia for Love

Non-fiction

Bless the Bees: The Pending Extinction of our Pollinators and What You Can Do to Stop It

A, Bee, See: Who are our Pollinators and Why are They in Trouble?

Save the Monarch Butterfly

For my Valentina,

Who never ceases to inspire me

The day the power of love overrules the love of power, the world will know peace.

-Mahatma Gandhi

1

A glint of orange bounced off the arched windows of the building across Anacapa Street, as Brent Marks exited through the tall wooden portals of the Santa Barbara courthouse. The old courthouse seemed to have a soul. The soul of every jurist who'd ever made an argument between the tall walls of each formidable courtroom. The soul of every man who'd ever sat before a jury of his peers in judgment since 1927, when it first opened its doors.

How he dreamed of doing another grand trial in the old Spanish colonial building. Brent had spent the first 15 years of his 20 year career paying his dues leading up to that moment, doing bankruptcies, divorces and drunk driving cases, but since then he had earned the right to take the cases he wanted – cases of social importance.

As he strolled down De La Guerra to the small office on quaint State Street where he had hung his shingle 20 years earlier, Brent inhaled the fresh ocean air and thanked himself for deciding on Santa Barbara. It was a refreshing break from the bustle of smog-bound Los Angeles, where he would have been an ant scurrying amongst thousands of other ants, each trying to make a name for themselves in the law business. Santa Barbara was a small town, which can sometimes be an impediment to a newcomer, but during his "dues paying days" he had made a name for himself, and established a thriving private practice.

Brent turned left on State Street, feeling the privilege of being able to walk to and from his work. He imagined State Street 100 years ago, with the Wells Fargo stage coach barreling through, and the town growing up around the route. It was the perfect match for his heritage.

His father was an immigrant from Spain. Jose Marquez had changed the family name to Marks, to avoid the stereotypes that he felt were cast on the family by people who thought they were Mexican. Brent could have passed for Mexican himself, with his dark brown hair. His hazel eyes often looked brown, but he was much taller than most Mexicans. He was fluent in Spanish, which had helped him in the old days when he was a "poor man's lawyer." The Spaniards had tamed this land and now it was Brent's turn. He loved Santa Barbara.

He had made it to his State Street office just in time to check messages and make sure everything was in order for the big weekend. No work, only play and relaxation for the next 48 hours. As he entered the office, Melinda Powers, his secretary, looked worried. It was unusual for her to be there past quitting time on a Friday.

"Hey Mimi, what's wrong?" Brent asked her.

"You've got a call waiting. I told him you weren't in, but he said he'd wait."

"Who is it?"

"I don't know, he won't say. He's really weird, Mr. Marks."

"Why don't we let him just die on hold then?"

"I think you should answer."

Brent entered his office, sat down behind his plush mahogany desk, and picked up the phone.

"Hello, this is Brent Marks."

The eerie voice on the other end was cold and inhuman. "Do you know how fast a bullet goes, Counselor?" it asked.

"Who is this?"

"Seventeen hundred feet per second. At that velocity, it will crack open your skull and

3

splatter your brains all over your wall like a watermelon being hit by a sledge hammer." The caller cackled like a wounded chicken.

Brent quickly switched on the recording device to the receiver. He had bought that baby to record threats from ex-husbands whose wives had obtained restraining orders against them, but which Brent had always refused to dismiss, even in cases of so called "reconciliation."

"I don't think I got your name, mister?"

The voice responded with a maniacal chuckle, which turned into a full blown belly laugh, like Vincent Price in the final stanza of Michael Jackson's *Thriller.*

"No judge in the world can stop a bullet, Counselor. No piece of paper can do that."

"This conversation is really interesting, but if I don't have your name, I…"

"Think hard."

"I'm not going to play games with you."

"Oh, this is not a game. I assure you. I'm just giving you a little preview. Wherever you go, I'll be there. When you're at the corner at Starbucks, having your mocha grande in the morning before going to court, I'll be there. You won't see me, but I'll be there. All it takes is one shot – one shot in the head." The phone vibrated from the eerie laughter.

"And why would you want to shoot me?"

"I am a servant of the Lord, Counselor. I do His work."

"You're saying that you're going to kill me, because God told you so?" Without answering, the caller went into a sermon, like an evangelist preacher trying to convert a world full of infidels.

"Vengeance is mine, I will repay, sayeth the Lord! When justice is done, it is a joy to the righteous but terror to evildoers. I am your terror, Counselor. I am the hand of the Lord and I will strike you down!"

Suddenly, Brent realized who this character could be. Last year, he took on a case for Felipe Sanchez, who had rented a house from a crazy religious fanatic named Joshua Banks. When Banks found out that Sanchez had moved in his girlfriend, all hell broke loose. "I won't have fornication in my house!" Banks decreed. Sanchez ignored him and three days later, came home to find himself locked out of his house and all his furniture thrown out on the street. When Brent succeeded in getting the police to open the house, Banks turned off the utilities, and Sanchez sued. Thanks to a little known provision in the Civil Code, daily damages were awarded to Sanchez at trial which allowed him to take his judgment, levy it against the house, and become the owner of it. Justice can be hell for some people.

"Threatening my life is a felony, Mr. Banks," said Brent, "Do you really want to go to prison?"

"Do you think I care about your court? Your prison? There is only one lawgiver and judge, and that is the Lord God! Judge not, that you not be judged, sayeth the Lord. Man does not have the right to sit in judgment of his fellow man."

"You're not God, Mr. Banks." Ignoring him, Banks pressed on.

"Your judgment has been pronounced, Counselor. And I'm afraid there is no chance for a pardon. The punishment is death."

Brent heard a click, followed by the dull dead sound of dial tone. It was now after 5:30 p.m. on a Friday. There was no way he could get a restraining order until the court opened on Monday morning, and the police would refuse to do anything about it unless he had one.

"Mims, I've gotta work you this weekend."

"Oh, boss, it's my sister's birthday tomorrow and we planned to go to Solvang to see *Legally Blonde*. Do I have to?" she pleaded, batting her eyelashes over her powder blue eyes. Melinda was 20 something, a little ditzy, attractive, with auburn brown hair, and had a huge crush on the boss. But Brent had long since made it clear that their relationship would be strictly business. Still, that did not prevent her from using her feminine wiles whenever she had the occasion, or, in this case, the need.

"Sorry, but if I don't get a restraining order against this crazy Joshua Banks, I'm afraid you may not have a boss by Monday."

"That was Banks? Oh, I remember that guy. He's nuts."

"You can do it at home. I'll dictate it now and drop it by your house in about two hours. But I need it by Sunday night. Court opens at 8:30."

"Okay boss, you can count on me."

It was a good thing that Brent had not yet made any plans for the weekend, because it would be reserved for writing up a motion for a restraining order and trying to stay alive long enough for the Court to grant it and the Sheriff to serve it.

2

Two years earlier...

April Marsh knew when she rang the bell at the security gate outside her parent's lavish home in Hope Ranch that something was wrong. The drive from L.A was a long one, and she had been stuck in slow weekend traffic all the way from Thousand Oaks. She was tired and worried. Mom and Dad had not answered her calls, and would usually check in with her if they were planning on going somewhere, at least to ask for a dog sitter for their two mutts. All was still and quiet – no dogs barking – just the gentle sound of the waves lapping against the shore in the back of the property. An eerie fog had begun to shroud the large home; a heavy shadow that seemed to hide it from the rest of the world. As she stood outside the grounds of the estate, April looked more like a real estate agent than an investigative journalist from Los Angeles, via New York, where she had learned the trade. She was dressed in a black blouse, light grey ankle cut trousers, and perched on high heeled black Christian Louboutins, as she brushed her long blonde hair out of her turquoise green eyes, trying to make sense of the silence.

April rang the gate bell again – no answer. She pushed against the gate and it creaked open, giving way. *Strange,* she thought. *Mom and Dad always keep the gate locked.* April walked through the unkempt garden, once finely manicured by a team of gardeners. Since Dad lost most of his money in the stock market crash of 2008, the gardeners were the first to go. What was once a series of plush flowerbeds bursting with color was now a few patches of flowers with wild vines and weeds weaving through them. Mom wasn't much into gardening, with all the added responsibilities of cleaning a house once maintained by maids resting on her shoulders.

April proceeded through the courtyard, to the once grand entrance, which was now collecting curled paint chips from the decaying door. As she reached out and knocked on the door, it squeaked open slowly; a sound you would imagine a coffin with rusty old hinges would make in a horror film; and that sound, combined with the dead silence that followed brought on a creepy chill and adrenaline rush from that uneasy feeling that something was not quite right.

"Mom?" she called, as she entered the travertine paved foyer. The call seemed to echo and reverberate throughout the house. *Maybe they're out in the back,* she thought. There was a lot of land out there, which led all the way to the cliffs overlooking the ocean. It would be virtually impossible to hear anything from the end of the property.

"Dad?" she called, her voice once again meeting with dead silence. Then her shuffling toe made contact with something soft and fleshy. She looked down in horror at the lifeless body of their German shepherd, Baron, who looked like his head had been crushed. She recoiled in horror, dropping her purse. Surging, panicking, she ran into the living room, almost spraining her ankle, as she landed on the side of her right heel. She kicked off her shoes and ran into the family room. "Mom!" she yelled, crying, trying to cover as much ground in the big house as she could. *Why did they ever get this big house?* was just one of the thoughts flying through her head, as her eyes quickly scanned each room she ran through in panic. Then, realizing she had dropped her purse, she quickly ran back to get it, sweeping it up with one arm and continued her search. *How stupid it was to drop it.*

"Mom!"

"Dad!"

Nobody was in the kitchen, the dining room, the downstairs guest bedroom. April turned and headed for the stairs. There, at the landing, was the limp body of Daisy, their Weimaraner, her tongue hanging out loosely, surrounded by a slick pool of her own blood. April screamed, but her fleeting grief for her precious Daisy was overpowered by the panic she felt for her parents. The realization that they were probably dead was competing with the hope that they were still alive, somewhere, and that they could be helped.

April bounded up the stairs, and into her parents' bedroom, and came face to face with the battered remains of her mother, propped up against the wall like a rag doll, Her lifeless eyes were open with her face frozen in her last moment of terror, her bruised and battered arms lay to the side, and her legs were splayed out in front of her bloodied torso. April could hardly recognize her mom, whose reddened bloodied head resembled that of a voodoo doll. She turned away from the scene, the blood drained from her brain, and she turned a pasty white. Hunched over with her hands on her knees, April choked and threw up. The blood returned to her brain, she stood up and tried to catch her breath, hyperventilating and exhaling with every profound sob, like she had a chronic case of the hiccups.

Turning from the ghastly grotesque scene of her mother's murder, April screamed from the gut for her father, stretching the one syllable into an entire sentence, "Daad!" and ran into the corridor, bumping her arm on the door frame as she did, her purse sliding from her shoulder down to the crook of her elbow.

She found him in his study, slumped over his computer desk. He had been bludgeoned and his blood was spattered everywhere. "Oh, dad…" she expelled, sadly, summoning the courage in her grief to feel around his bloody neck for a pulse as a last expenditure of hope.

A faint pulse! She thrust open her purse, snatched her cell phone and punched 911, while the purse fell to the floor, and spewed the rest of its contents.

"911, what is your emergency?"

"My…mother…has been murdered….my dad…is still alive…please send someone fast! 5689 Marina Drive…please help us!"

3

The upcoming client had Brent intrigued. Her matter was a potential wrongful predatory lending case against one of the largest New York banks, which had taken over one of the nation's largest mortgage banks, rumored to have committed more fraud than Charles Ponzi and Bernie Madoff put together. It was the type of case that could put him over the top, not only financially, but professionally, and he squirmed in his black leather high back chair as he impatiently waited for her. He was too anxious and it was too close to her appointment time to start any new project, even a letter.

"Did she call in?" he called to Melinda, in the next room.

"You asked me that twice already. She's not even late yet."

"Okay, sorry. Well let me know right away if she calls in."

"I'm sure she'll be here on time. It's an important case."

Brent knew that, or at least he hoped it was. Oftentimes, clients would think that they had the greatest case in the world, and those clients can be a lawyer's worst enemy. They do their own legal research, without the benefit of the three years' training you get in law school, not to mention the 20 years of on the job training in practice. They make suggestions on the pleadings that you have to cross out and often confuse you. And, worst of all, they usually come up with something like, "You know, I have some legal training. I took business law in high school, and I can save you a lot of time by writing the pleadings myself. You can just check them over and edit them." If looking over an amateur's work isn't bad enough, they then expect a reduction in the fees for their "generous contribution." Brent's primary rule in dealing with clients was, *It's your case, but I'm the lawyer. If you don't trust my work, hire someone else.*

Some people don't like lawyers, that is, until they need them. But, as Charles Dickens said, *if there were no bad people, there would be no good lawyers.*

A lawyer is your "friend in need." Lawyers have a different way of thinking; analytical thinking that does not incorporate the emotional side of the issue. Granted, a lawyer can and should care about your case, but when the chips are down you don't want him to blubber about it in court.

You want a clear, objective analysis that he can argue to a judge. Emotions are reserved for juries and, in that case, a good lawyer can really lay them on when the time is right, better than the best Academy Award winning actor. Brent never took on a case he didn't think he could win.

4

Melinda walked in, with a smirky grin on her face, to announce the arrival of the client. "You're gonna like this one," she said. Brent made a face to her that said, "Be professional," and responded, "Please show her in."

The woman was stunning. At about 30, golden blonde hair, forest green eyes, and with an exquisite figure, April Marsh could arouse any man on earth better than 100 milligrams of Viagra. Brent sized her up right away, keeping his emotions at bay, of course, and his eyes away from her ample, but not overwhelming breasts, which seemed to peek at him from her V-neck blouse.

"Brent Marks," he said, extending his hand. She took it. Her hand was warm and pleasant, but the handshake firm. "April Marsh."

"Please have a seat."

April sat down gently in one of the classic wooden chairs across from Brent's desk, crossing her legs at the knee in one continuous smooth motion, resting her hands on her pleated skirt. The chairs were comfortable enough for a conversation of the required length, but not padded, so as not to encourage a longer visit than was necessary.

"How can I help you?" asked Brent.

"As I told you on the phone, I'm looking for the right lawyer to handle my father's case against Prudent Bank."

"Yes, your father is incapacitated."

"That's right. He was almost killed, and now he can't communicate."

"And you've been appointed already as his conservator?"

"Yes."

"I looked at the materials you sent over to me. Of course, I would have to review all of the files, but its looks like when the bank bought the assets of Tentane Mutual after the FDIC seizure, your father's mortgage was not properly assigned to the mortgage backed securities trust that was supposed to be one of the assets."

Before the 2008 mortgage crisis, thousands of subprime real estate loans on over-appraised real estate were assigned to mortgage pools and then resold to investors as mortgage backed securities. When U.S. home prices declined sharply after peaking in 2006, it became difficult for borrowers to refinance their loans. As adjustable rate mortgages began to increase in monthly payments, mortgage delinquencies soared, causing mortgage backed securities to lose most of their value. This, in turn, led to what is known as the financial crisis of 2008; the worst financial crisis since the Great Depression.

"Yes, they tried to slip it in with a forged assignment three years after the closing date of the Trust."

"I saw that. The assignment of the deed of trust was signed by Prudent Bank, who was not even authorized to assign to the Trust."

"And it was a robo-signing."

Robo-signing was a common practice during the years leading to the 2008 financial crisis, where numerous low level bank employees would sign important documents, as officers of the bank, often with forged notary signatures. Brent could see the prima facie elements of a solid mortgage fraud case against the bank.

"The branch president talked my father into the loan," she continued, "to get him back on his feet after he lost most of his capital in the stock market. Then, when the loan adjusted and the payments doubled, he talked him into going behind on his mortgage payments so he could qualify for a loan modification because he said it would be easier than a refi."

"But he never got the modification."

"That's right, only a foreclosure notice, and now he can't pay at all." April's lip quivered, and tears welled up in her eyes.

"What's the name of the branch manager?"

"Steve Bernstein. He's a vice president of Prudent Bank now."

"Ms. Marsh…"

"April."

"April, my preliminary review tells me you have a potential case of mortgage fraud here, and we may be able to have the court declare that Prudent Bank has no power to collect on the loan or foreclose on the deed of trust."

"I know, but that's not why I came to you." Brent looked puzzled.

"I don't understand."

"I came to you because of your landmark case against Prudent Bank last year. My mother was murdered, Mr. Marks, and my father was beat within an inch of his life."

"I know. I remember the case. The police never identified a suspect."

"I know who did it."

"You do?"

"Well, I know who ordered it, but I can't prove it, but you can."

"Wait a minute, I'm a civil lawyer. You came to me to discuss the case against the bank."

"The bank did it." April's eyes were trained straight on Brent's. "I know you may think I'm crazy, but I know the bank is behind my mother's murder."

"And how does that tie into your mortgage fraud case?"

"Mr. Marks…"

"Brent."

"Brent, do you remember the OJ Simpson case?"

"Yes I do."

"Did you have any doubt that OJ was responsible for Nicole Brown and Ron Goldman's murder?"

"None whatsoever. But he was acquitted."

"That's right, but he lost the civil case for wrongful death. I'm here because you proved in the Carson case that Prudent's employees perjured themselves in Court, right?"

"Yes."

"And that they committed mail fraud and wire fraud in the process of foreclosing on your client's home?"

"Yes."

"Well, aren't murder and attempted murder predicate acts under RICO?" RICO, the Racketeer Influenced and Corrupt Organizations Act, was a federal statute that Brent had used against the bank in his landmark wrongful foreclosure case.

"Look, Ms. Marsh."

"April."

"April, I'm not sure you came to the right lawyer for this."

"Oh, I'm absolutely sure I did. My mother is dead. My father will probably die soon. I don't give a damn about the house. I just want those bastards to pay for what they did to my parents." Her bottom lip, the one that was quivering before, was absolutely stiff. The telltale sign of the problem client who wanted to sue for "the principle" began to rear its head in Brent's mind.

"What gives you the idea the bank is behind your mother's murder?"

"My father was the principal witness in a grand jury investigation against the bank. All the other witnesses were scared off. He wasn't. Most people, faced with two difficult choices, prefer not to choose at all. My family is not one to back down from a conflict." Brent could see that.

"Unfortunately, violence has a way of overpowering even the strongest of wills," she added.

"I'll look at the case and make a full evaluation. If I think I can win, I'll take it. That's all I can promise you."

"I left the files up front with your secretary."

"Great, I'll give you a call after I evaluate the case, but I have one ground rule with all my clients."

"What's that?"

"It's your case, but if I take it, as long as I'm on it, I run it. Is that agreed?"

"Yes, so long as you agree that we have a RICO case and that murder is one of the predicate acts." April was tough. She would make a terrible damsel in distress.

"Like I said, I will evaluate the case and let you know." Brent stood up, showing her that the interview was over. April stood up as well, and shook his hand.

"Thank you, Brent. I'm glad I found the right lawyer."

"I haven't taken the case yet."

As she turned to leave, and Brent watched the swish of her hips, he almost lost sight of his rules. April turned her silky blonde head, her eyes smiling. "You will," she said.

5

Brent set aside the rest of the day to dig through cases. In the old days, you had to go to the law library to do legal research, or buy hundreds of law books, at the cost of thousands of dollars per month. Now, thanks to the Internet, which leveled the playing field, for less than $100 per month, Brent had access to all the legal authorities he needed, and all it took was his computer and a lot of time.

Brent actually had a social life, but he was between girlfriends at the moment, so he plowed into his work. As his late mentor, Charles Stinson, used to say, "Your first mistress is the law." Of course, he said that when Brent was too busy fooling around to prepare for a joint case he and Charles were working on until the last minute. Then, early on the morning of the trial, they were both in the office together, copying exhibits and preparing testimony, because Charles also valued his play time.

RICO, the Racketeering Influenced Corrupt Organizations Act, was first enacted in 1970 by Congress to take a bite out of organized crime in the 60's, but it also can be used to bring a civil action, and that is where Brent focused his research. Since its enactment, RICO cases had been brought against the Hells Angels Motorcycle Club, famous mafia crime families like the Gambinos and Luccheses, and even business tycoon Michael Milken. But most civil RICO cases never got past the pleading stages. Big business committed big crimes, but they also hired big firms to defend them, and spent big money to get the best defense. Most RICO claims did not have a chance.

The law was a tool. It was complicated, but being your own lawyer was worse than being your own surgeon. Lawyers are expensive, and powerful people can afford more of them than the common man. To go up against Prudent Bank was no easy task for a one-man firm like Brent's.

To make a case under RICO, Brent would have to plead that Prudent Bank was a criminal enterprise, and that it had committed at least two serious crimes (predicate acts) as part of the operation of the enterprise. Certainly murder and attempted murder were among the top offenses that could be alleged, but Brent thought it a little far-fetched that a bank could be accused of murder. However, companies do not exist independently of the people who run them, and people do commit murder for many various reasons.

Brent had seen enough fraud in April's files on the part of both Tentane Mutual Bank as well as a cover-up by Prudent Bank to stick Prudent with a nice fat mortgage fraud claim, but going after them for RICO was a bigger stretch. The last thing he wanted was for the Court to throw out his case on a motion to dismiss, or for the judge to get a bad impression about it to begin with.

Tentane and Prudent had falsified documents. They didn't bother having notaries actually sign and witness documents, as required by law. They just stamped the notary's stamps on the documents and had employees in their mortgage processing factories in more than 15 states forge the notaries' names. That was known as "robo-signing," and, April, being an investigative reporter, had already obtained expert handwriting analysis and records to prove the assignments of the mortgage were forgeries. She also had a forensic report that showed a faulty chain of title of documents on the Marshes' mortgage. Prudent Bank knew about the fraud, yet proceeded with foreclosure like nothing was done wrong.

What it meant to Mr. Marsh was that Prudent Bank, who had purchased the assets of Tentane

Mutual by an agreement with the government on the eve of the FDIC seizure, did not have the legal right to foreclose on the Marsh home.

Prudent had already paid millions of dollars in fines to numerous government agencies and investors for their deceptive mortgage loan origination and fraudulent securitization practices. They knew about the problems with the faulty assignments and forgeries, but covered them up and continued to record false documents to try to bury the massive fraud after they took over Tentane Mutual.

Since they used the U.S. Mail and made interstate telephone calls in connection with their cover up, Brent surmised that he could hang a RICO case against them by alleging the predicate acts of mail fraud (the U.S. Mail) and wire fraud (the interstate telephone calls). That way, he didn't have to prove a murder case. But now he had to sell this idea to April.

***

Brent looked at the clock. It was already 10 p.m. He picked up the phone to call his buddy, Rick Penn, who was also his investigator.

"Dude, I think I've got a juicy case for you," said into the phone.

"You've gotta be kidding me, it's 10 freakin' p.m. If you want to talk about it, get down to Sonny's and we'll talk about it over a drink."

Sonny's was Rick's favorite bar. State Street may be charming during the day, but at night, the lower part of it, near the Santa Barbara Pier, got pretty wild. Sonny's was one of the bars on the lower side that always seemed to always be full, even on the weekdays.

"I'll be there in twenty," said Brent, and hung up the phone.

6

Sonny's was always packed and the fact that it was Thursday night made no difference. The cops had already parked some squad cars on State Street to prepare for their post bar-closing drunk driving dragnet, so Brent had been smart and walked there from his office. It was about ten blocks, but they were short blocks. Santa Barbara itself was a small town, only 42 square miles, but it had the longest south facing coastline on the west coast, which was beautiful it was referred to as the "American Riviera."

Brent planned to take a cab home after the meeting. He knew only too well California's DUI laws. There was no way he would be caught driving under the influence of alcohol, even though he knew all the prosecutors in the city – especially because he knew all the prosecutors in the city.

As was typical with most of the bars and bar and grills downtown, Sonny's had an outdoor seating area on the sidewalk. Brent could see that it was completely full of after-work partiers as he approached. Men in slacks who had shed their ties and jackets, and women in loosened dress wear toasted each other and celebrated being away from the office. Since it was only a few blocks from the coast, it made for a frosty evening even on a summer night, but the peeps at Sonny's didn't care. They were insulated from the inside out and feeling warm and fuzzy all over. Sonny's kick ass sound system was so good, Brent could swear it was really Shakira singing instead of her recording of "Whenever, Wherever," when he walked in.

Rick was sitting at the bar. He was easy to pick out in a crowd because he was the tallest guy at the bar. He was always easy to spot, for that matter, because he was always the tallest guy anywhere. When Brent first started hanging out with him, it was kind of intimidating because he didn't quite know where to look. He wanted to look up because he eventually had to put his head down, and he didn't want Rick to think he was looking at his crotch. The other thing was, it's usually nice to make eye contact with someone you're having a conversation with. Seated at the bar, it was a lot easier. He didn't have to strain his neck.

Rick smiled, and put out his hand for the "thumb to thumb" handshake, which Brent tackled with experience as he slid onto the bar chair. Rick was an ex-FBI agent, retired from the Bureau for about five years, about 56 years old, 13 years Brent's senior, with greying hair that still fully covered his head and, although he tried to look cool, he could never shake that "G-Man look," which was a combination between "GQ" and nerd. He definitely looked better in a suit than the long baggy grey shorts and black Def Leppard T-shirt he wore.

Rick had started out with the LAPD, and was hired out by the Bureau after putting in about five years hard work as a street cop, and then spent the next ten years of his career in the Bureau's LA office until the Santa Barbara position opened. His buddies in LA used to joke that he went "on vacation" when he transferred to Santa Barbara. For Rick, it was a step closer to the perfect retirement. He now worked as a private eye to supplement his retirement income from the government.

They had met about ten years before, when Brent was taking just about any case for money, just to survive in private practice. Rick had walked into the office, fully suited, and presented himself as Special Agent Penn of the FBI. Brent had almost pissed himself, wondering if this G-Man had come to arrest him for something. It turned out that he just needed a general education on securities, and Brent was well versed in them, having recently settled a big securities fraud lawsuit.

"What's goin' on big dog?" Rick asked.

"Hey dude."

Rick flagged down the bartender, a lanky young guy, who leaned over to take the order.

"Whatcha drinkin'?" asked Rick.

"I'll have one of those chick's martinis."

"Cosmo," Rick said to the bartender, who nodded and went to work on it.

"Drinkin' the chick's drinks, means you're getting horny, dude," said Rick.

"You know me, I'm always horny." Rick laughed. "Look, I need you to take a look at a case for me," said Brent.

"Who's the client? Gotta know so there's no conflict."

"April Marsh."

"Doncha mean March April?" Rick prided himself as the master of puns. Of course, after a couple of drinks, his corny jokes got even better, or so he thought.

"Very funny."

"So, what's she look like?"

"Rick, come on, man."

"No, you come on. One to ten, a five? Seven? Is she hot?"

"Rick, I didn't come here to talk chicks."

"Since when do we not talk chicks? Plus we're in a bar for fuck's sake. What else do guys talk about in a bar?"

"Dude, I can't get involved with a client."

"Oh, so she *is* hot?"

"Can't say."

"What? What happened, did your dick go on vacation or something?" What's she look like?" Brent was stoic.

"Blonde hair?" asked Rick. Brent said nothing, giving it away. "Blue eyes? Green?" Again nothing. "Whoa, I'm on a roll now. Smokin' hot body too, right?"

"If you must know…"

"I must."

"Yes, all of that." Rick whistled.

"Can we be serious now?" asked Brent. The bartender slid the pink martini to Brent across the sticky counter. Rick pointed to his own glass with a "pouring motion" and the bartender topped it up.

"Serious is too boring."

"It's no boring case."

"Yeah, you told me." He covered his mouth, as if to yawn. "Financial fraud, whoopee!"

"This is different."

"How so?"

"Her parents' house was in foreclosure, Prudent Bank – major fraud.

"So?"

"Her mother was murdered. Father beat within an inch of his life."

"You told me. And?"

"She says the bank VP did it."

"Why would a bank VP want to murder her mother?"

"That was my initial reaction too. Seems the bank was up against a Grand Jury investigation for all their dirty little mortgage dealings and the parents were witnesses."

"Now that is interesting. Well, banks are the biggest mafia, you know, except for the government of course."

"Of course."

"Calls for a toast," Rick said, lifting his glass. Brent took the cue and raised his class as well. "Give me everything and I'll sniff around for you." Rick slammed his drink as Brent took a sip from his martini.

"Come by the office tomorrow afternoon. Melinda should have your copies of the files ready by then," said Brent.

"Don't have to talk me into it. That Melinda is one helluva fox."

"Dude, nobody says fox anymore."

"Yeah, well nobody says dude anymore either. Hey, whatever happened with that nut case and the restraining order?"

"Joshua Banks? They served him on Monday."

"Yeah?"

"Yeah, I told the Sheriff he was dangerous, so they asked the cops for help. They brought out the whole freakin' SWAT team – served the guy at gunpoint and everything – he even gave up his whole gun collection."

"No shit."

"No shit. I think that one is under control."

"Just watch your back, man. You never know."

"I know."

"And Brent…"

"Yeah?"

"You know you can always call me if it gets too hairy."

"I know, thanks."

"No need." Brent knew that was true. The mark of a good friend. Someone who asked for nothing, and gave everything. Someone you could call up at 3 in the morning who would never be pissed off at you. And he could do the same.

7

April was ecstatic when Brent told her the news on the phone. "Now, we have to investigate, we have to prepare..." she said.

"Wait a minute. Remember, I told you I run the case?"

"Yes, of course."

"Your role is to provide information when I need it, not to investigate. You've done a great job so far, but I have my own investigator who used to work for the FBI."

"Okay, well then we should meet to discuss the case."

Normally, Brent liked to have as little client contact as possible. Talk to the client, find out what is necessary to find out, get paid and go to work. With April, it would be easy to make an exception, but that could turn into breaches of other rules he had set for himself, so he decided to play by the book, instead of by the seat of his pants.

"I should have you sign the contract and, of course, we need to settle the matter of my retainer."

"No problem. When can I come by to sign and drop off a check?"

This was the exception to the infrequent contact rule. Clients with checks were always welcome, no matter how much of a pain in the ass they may be. If a client was holding a check, Brent could listen to the same story for the third time with the patience of Job. He even had a box of Kleenex on his desk for the teary-eyed moments.

Brent had heard every story that could be imagined in the human experience over the last 20 years – women who were beaten by their husbands, parents who molested their children, women who wanted to be men, men who wanted to be women, same sex couples who wanted a 'divorce.' The variations on human misery that he had witnessed could keep a psychiatrist busy for life.

***

When April came by to sign the agreement and drop off the check for the retainer, she was dressed to make an impression as usual, in smart black slacks and a red silk shirt. Melinda showed her in, taking silent wardrobe notes.

"You look wonderful," Brent told her. "Please have a seat."

"Thank you," April said, sitting down. She dug around in her purse and pulled out the check, handing it to Brent. He accepted it, said "thank you," and put it on the desk, like it was not as important as it was. Then, Brent slid the two page retainer agreement over to her.

"So, once I sign this, you take over, right?"

"Yes, it will then be in my hands."

"Before I do, I just want to be sure of one thing. I have your word that you will take the murder allegation seriously, right?"

"We can still plead RICO without it, but, if there is a shred of probable cause that Bernstein had anything to do with your mother's murder, we will plead it and try to prove it."

It was Voltaire who said that *all murderers had to be punished unless they kill in large numbers to the sound of trumpets.* If you believed the Bible, the first murder was committed by the victim's brother. We were put on the earth for so short a time. It was absolutely unconscionable for someone to arbitrarily decide that our time was up, and to make it so. Brent vowed to make sure that if he and Rick discovered who murdered April's mother and attempted to murder her father, they would be punished. No extra charge.

8

Charles Stinson used to tell Brent, "Nothing is easy," and, with respect to legal work, that was absolutely true. Most people had no appreciation of what went into a letter or a legal brief; they only saw the result. To get to that result was a tedious process, of legal research to find the law, analyzing the facts, and then applying the law to those facts in a concise legal argument. Legal arguments were like fingerprints. No two were ever completely alike. That was why the bar examination was so tough - only about 40% of people who took it passed it – and even less on the first try.

Brent had been working on the complaint for about a week, while Rick sniffed around. Night and day, he toiled at the office, thinking about each critical piece of the case and putting together allegations that were supported by his research. The case would be filed in federal court, and the bank would hire the best legal team they could to try to quash the complaint on a motion to dismiss. Everything had to be carefully worded and every cause of action carefully supported by the appropriate law.

As a provisional remedy, Brent would ask the court for a preliminary injunction to stall the foreclosure sale until the case could be finalized. In the case, he would ask for the court to declare that the mortgage, or deed of trust, as it was called, was void, because it was not assigned to the Trust pool of mortgages by the closing date of the Trust. A technical argument, but one that had some limited precedent.

Because the note and deed of trust were void, Prudent Bank had no right to collect on them as the servicer of the loan, as the mortgage had never been properly assigned to the Trust. He would plead fraud and bad faith, and that the bank was violating the Fair Debt Collection Practices Act.

But, the weakest link was RICO. That was the part the bank would work the hardest to throw out; not necessarily because they were guilty of murder, but because they were guilty of bank fraud and RICO carried a punitive damage penalty of three times the actual damages you could prove. It was like 2-1 odds at the horse track.

***

To Brent, it seemed like he had just finished breakfast at 7 am, came to the office, and checked his email, but it was coming up on 4 pm and he had not even eaten lunch yet. He was developing a headache from eye strain. Brent knew there were others besides April and Melinda counting on him. There was also Calico, his orange and white cat. He decided to take off early, which meant that he would pack up his laptop and head home, taking a short break to feed and pet the cat before getting back to work.

The phone rang just as Brent was leaving the office. Brent generally hated talking on the phone, and considered it a nuisance, except for the conveyance of absolutely essential information, which was better done by email anyway, so before Melinda announced who it was, he said, "Take a message."

"Mr. Marks, I think you should take this one. It's Mr. Penn."

Brent picked up the phone. "What's up, Rick?"

"Can you come down to the cop shop right away? I've gotta show you something."

"Does this mean I can put the 'M' word in the complaint?"

"Come down and see for yourself. Meet me in homicide."

Brent packed up his laptop, said good-bye to Melinda, and headed for the police station.

9

The Santa Barbara County Sheriff had jurisdiction over Hope Ranch which, technically, was not within the city boundaries. Their office on Calle Real was about an eight minute drive from the office. Brent met Rick there along with William Branson, a no-nonsense detective with the homicide division. Rick knew William from his days at the FBI. William was dressed in his usual uniform – black slacks with a white shirt that needed a little extra bleach on the next wash, and a tie that looked like it was retired in the 70's. Anyway, it matched the style of his dyed hair comb over. After a round of handshakes and introductions, the three got down to business, which centered around a few boxes of materials that were spread out on William's desk.

"Here's what I wanted to show you," Rick proudly said, holding up a report with a bunch of color coded strands.

"What is it?" asked Brent.

"It's a polymerase chain reaction report on a hair fiber found at the crime scene," chimed in Branson, as if that was supposed to mean something to Brent.

"Guys, I'm a lawyer, not a scientist, tell me in plain English what we're looking at and why I'm here," said Brent.

"This is a result of DNA profiling done on the hair found at the crime scene," said Branson. "There was a sampling that didn't match either victim."

"Meaning that the murderer, or someone with the murderer, lost a hair during the struggle," said Brent.

"Very good," said Rick. "We think that April's mom fought back."

"Great work guys," said Brent. "Now all we have to do is find the murderer and we can prove it was him."

"Yeah, that is the hard part," said Rick. "Bernstein doesn't have a criminal record, so we've got nothing to go on. But it's a start."

"Look, I'm going to head home. You guys call me if you find anything else, okay?" Brent left the station, a little peeved at Rick, but he couldn't fault his enthusiasm. He slipped behind the wheel of his blue Jaguar F-Type and peeled out of the parking lot.

* * *

If the human brain is really capable of having 60,000 to 80,000 thoughts per day, Brent was living proof, because he never stopped thinking. As he drove home, he had an epiphany and pulled over to the side. He took his cell phone out of his pocket and called Rick.

"Rick, April said Bernstein was a branch manager for Prudent before he made VP, right?"

"Right."

"What about before that?"

"What do you mean?"

"Before he was a branch manager, what did he do?"

"I don't know. Why?"

"Prudent Bank is a major bank. Most of those major banks have a drug testing policy. And some of them use hair follicles. Find out what lab does their testing and see if they save the samples."

"Oh shit, I see where you're going."

If the hair follicles from the drug testing were saved, Brent thought he may be able to obtain them in the discovery process, and then compare the DNA in the hair follicles with the hair found at the murder scene. But to get that far, they needed something more than just April's hunch, nor matter how strongly she felt about it.

10

Brent checked traffic in his rear view mirror and side mirrors routinely as he headed down the 101 freeway to home. Traffic was typical for a Wednesday afternoon, but there was something strange about it. A white Mustang about ten cars down seemed to be following his every move.

Either he was paranoid, or somebody was following him. To test the theory, Brent changed lanes. A few moments later, the white Mustang also changed lanes. If he was being followed, there was no way Brent wanted to give away where he lived, especially if it was some crazy nut like Joshua Banks. And if it was Banks, Bent wanted to make sure he nailed him on violating the restraining order, so Brent exited the freeway at Las Positas, and turned onto State Street. The white car was still behind him.

Brent turned left on Anapamu, parked alongside the courthouse, and called 911. The Santa Barbara police station was about a half block away, so it wouldn't take long for them to get there. The Mustang was still behind him, parked about a block down, and it looked like it had two occupants in it. Brent described the vehicle, as well as his suspicions that it was Banks, who had violated the restraining order, and sat tight for the cops.

About ten minutes later, two uniformed officers approached the white car on foot, from behind. They must have gone through the courthouse to sneak up on the occupants in the white car to detain them before they had a chance to pull away. When the two officers had the white car covered, another two, a man and a woman, approached Brent's car from the front.

"Good afternoon, sir," said the male officer. The female officer stood by, talking on her small two-way radio strapped to her shoulder.

"Afternoon, said Brent."

"Could I see your driver's license and registration please, sir?"

Brent didn't really like interacting with the police. They seemed more like machines than humans, and, let's face it, they are a civilian's army. An army whose soldiers dressed in costumes and walked and talked like robots, with guns strapped to their waist belts, always looking for an enemy. But he had called them, and, of course, they had to identify him to determine if he posed any threat to their safety.

"Of course," Brent replied, and presented his documents, including the restraining order, which he kept in his glove compartment, and the officer excused himself to talk to his partner. Then, they both returned.

"Sir, we've identified the suspects and neither one of them is the individual in your restraining order," said the male officer. Police officers always referred to people as "individuals."

"Did these individuals threaten you with violence in any way?"

"They were following me."

"But did they make any contact with you at all? Touch you or your car or communicate with you in any way?" Brent knew what was coming.

"No."

"Sir, I'm afraid that, without a restraining order against them, there is nothing we can do." Brent already knew that.

"I understand. Can you do me a favor please? Can you take their names and addresses for your report so I can find out who has been following me?"

"All that information will be in our report, sir, and you can obtain a copy from the station." The officer handed Brent a slip of paper. "This is the report reference number. Just give them that."

"Thank you," Brent said, as he watched the white Mustang roll by. The occupants in the car were white males. He couldn't see any other features as they drove by, trying not to look at him, but he could get all that information from the report.

"You're welcome, sir. Have a nice day," said the male officer, and the two of them walked away.

＊

Brent called Rick on the phone to tell him about the tail. He would pick up the report in the morning.

"Don't go straight home," Rick advised. "Take the scenic route and make sure nobody's following you."

Brent did, running all the way down busy State Street and turning right at the entrance to the Pier onto Shoreline Drive, passing the beautiful beach and coastline, all the while checking his mirrors for any sign of a tail. By the time he turned right on La Coronilla, he was sure that nobody had followed him.

Pulling up to his home on Harbor Hills Drive, the expansive view of the ocean and shoreline behind the house reminded him of why he had bought the place. It was always pleasant to come home to. Brent pressed the button to open the garage door, and pulled in.

＊

When Brent opened the front door, Calico greeted him right away. The orange and white cat with the round smiling face was as much a part of his home as the house itself. But there was something strange about her today. She seemed a bit nervous, flighty, and wasn't purring as usual.

"Hey Callie, what's wrong girl?" The cat flitted about, wagging her tail vigorously. Then Brent saw what had made her so nervous. In the middle of the living room, there was a stone. Underneath Calico's favorite windowsill were shards of broken glass.

Once he took a closer look, Brent could see that there was a paper attached to the stone. Brent went to the kitchen to put on some latex kitchen gloves so as not to disturb any evidence. He carefully untied the twine that held the paper wrapped tightly against the stone, and, holding only the edges of the corners, straightened it out so he could read it. It read, *Stay away from April Marsh.* Brent immediately called Rick. He was sure there would be no traces of fingerprints on the note, but you never know.

11

"No prints on the paper," Rick reported, as he kicked back in the client's chair and put his feet on Brent's desk.

"What a surprise," said Brent, adding "Get your grungy feet off my desk!"

The cops had spent over two hours at his house. It wasn't quite his idea of a quiet evening at home with the cat. Rick took his feet off the desk, and plopped them against the other client's chair.

"There's more bad news, I'm afraid."

"Great. Give it to me."

"Prudent Bank does have a drug screening policy, but they use blood tests, not hair follicles."

"Wonderful."

"But I've got the police report on the tail," Rick continued. "The car is registered to the driver, a Kevin Suskind, age 26, crack head, and his buddy, the passenger, was William Conlan, 30, a hefty body building freak. Any idea who these guys might be?"

"None at all."

"I'm going to talk to them and see what I can shake out. But first, I'm going to pay a visit to our Mr. Bernstein."

"What for?"

"If anything else, I can probably tell if he's guilty just by looking at him. Then we'll know if we're on a snipe hunt or not."

Rick had looked into the empty eyes of enough criminals (the murderous kind) to spot them right away. Brent had too, for that matter. When he first went into private practice, Charles Stinson got him on the private counsel list to defend parole violators when the public defender had overflows or declared a conflict. It was the eyes that gave them away. A hardened criminal cannot make eye contact with you, and, if you are able to look him in the eye, you see the windows to a most evil soul. Rick was used to it, having worked on serial killer task forces on more than one occasion, but it always gave Brent the chills.

12

Rick strolled into Steve Bernstein's Century City office at Prudent Bank unannounced, telling the receptionist he was from the FBI, and flashed his business card holder, which passed for a badge with most people. That usually broke all the ice. The office was an impressive spread, taking up the entire 37th floor of one of the Century Plaza Towers, with marble floors and wood paneling, befitting of any royal palace.

As he was shown into the "king's" office, an enormous spread with a glass wall showing a panoramic view of Los Angeles, Steve Bernstein met Rick with a fake smile and handshake. His palm was sweaty, like a horse after a quick run. Rick got a read on him right away as a phony, but his criminal radar was not going off.

"So what can we do for the FBI?" asked Bernstein. Rick continued to size him up. He was beady-eyed, cocky, short, balding, maybe in his early 40's, and tried to disguise his fear and anxiety with friendliness. He was the type of guy who never said, "hello." It was always "how are you." Rick didn't have a stomach for that type.

"Well, I'm here for a routine investigation, sir. It's about April Marsh."

"Marsh? Doesn't ring a bell." Bernstein drew his fuzzy eyebrows upward for a split second, causing short lines to appear across his forehead; a micro expression that gave away the fact that he was lying. Rick could see beads of perspiration forming on his neck and in between the hairs of his finely trimmed moustache.

"You sure? You wrote her father a mortgage loan; George Marsh?"

"George Marsh. Really don't recall that name either."

Bernstein leaned back in his chair and swallowed. Another micro expression. He was definitely lying.

"Well, let me show you a copy of the loan app. That should refresh your memory."

Rick put the file on Bernstein's desk. Bernstein glanced at it, and then looked away.

"That's my signature, still don't recall the name."

"Mr. Marsh was attacked two years ago, in his home. His wife was murdered."

Bernstein's knuckles were turning white, digging into the armrests of his leather judge's chair.

"I think I remember something about that from the newspapers. But, again, sorry, I just don't recall the person. Is there anything else I can do for you, Agent?"

"…Mr. Penn, here's my card in case you remember anything."

"Thank you," said Bernstein, shaking Rick's hand and taking the card. As Rick turned to leave, Bernstein remarked, "This says you're a private investigator. I thought you were from the FBI."

Rick turned and smiled. "I don't know whatever gave you that idea," he said, and left Bernstein standing in the middle of his panoramic office like a deer in headlights.

* * *

"So, is Bernstein our guy?" asked Brent.

"Don't know. Didn't get that far. Says he doesn't know Marsh. He's lying about that, though."

"What's your gut feeling?"

"He's definitely the criminal type. Whether he's a murderer, I can't really tell at this point."

"So, what next?"

"You want to file your complaint with the 'M' word, right?"

"Yeah."

"Well, then we look for evidence."

"Where?"

"Where do you think?"

"Whoa, what are you going to do?"

"You really wanna know?"

"No, no, I don't want to know anything."

"Good, I'll have hair samples for matching by the end of the week. But I don't think he's your guy. If he had anything to do with it, he probably hired a hit man."

"Why do you say that?"

"Just a gut feeling. He looks like the supervisor type; not one to get his hands dirty."

13

Rick Penn slipped through the back door of Steve Bernstein's house as if he was an experienced cat burglar, except his sights were not set on jewelry. He was going for Bernstein's hairbrush. He had made sure that Bernstein was not at home by a verifying call to his office. "Mr. Bernstein is in a meeting, may I take a message?" the receptionist had said. It should have been a quick, in and out affair. He would provide the sample, and, if it tested positive for the DNA from the murder scene, he would say he surreptitiously obtained it during his interview with Bernstein at his office. The brush was, as expected, in Bernstein's bathroom, but as he exited the bathroom with the sample, Rick found something that was not expected. There, standing in the corridor, was a masked man, his gloved hands holding a silencer equipped, Glock 9mm, trained at Rick's heart.

"Move," said the man.

Rick thought, in an instant, of possible routes of escape. There were none. Anything he tried would result in his being mortally wounded. So he tried a bluff.

"You can't shoot me here, Bernstein. My partners know where I am and if I don't call in to them in the next ten minutes, they'll be all over you."

"Nice try. Now move."

The masked man's eyes were as locked on Rick's as his weapon was on his chest. He was a cold blooded killer, no doubt about it. This was no bluff. Rick shuffled forward.

"Put your hands on your head and turn around."

Rick did as instructed, although he loathed the idea of not being able to watch the man's moves.

"Down the hallway."

Rick did as he was told, all the while looking for a way to escape.

"Now turn right through the door."

It was the door to the garage. Rick hesitated. The walls and floor were covered with heavy plastic. This was a dead end he would never escape. He had to make a move now to save himself, or he never would. Knowing that Bernstein or whomever it was would not risk shooting him in the corridor and spill his blood where it could later be used as evidence, Rick made a ballsy move. He turned to face his attacker.

"What the fuck are you doing?" questioned the man. But, before the question had a chance to linger in the air, Rick attacked. He reached for the weapon to disarm it, but the man took a step back. The muffled metallic ping of the bullet speeding through the silencer was the last thing that Richard Penn ever heard.

14

Brent awoke to the music of the birds chirping on the hillside of his Santa Barbara getaway. Calico, sensing that he was awake, jumped up on the bed, climbed onto his chest, and purred in harmony to the birds as she rubbed her whiskers against his face. A wonderful display of affection, but it was hardly pleasant to have a mouthful of cat fur first thing in the morning. Brent got out of bed, and Calico leaped out, making a beeline for the kitchen, where she pleaded for breakfast. Brent brushed his teeth, then grabbed his cell phone and turned on the sound on his way to the kitchen. *That's strange,* he thought. *No message from Rick.* Of course, Rick would not have given him the details, but he would have reported back whether he had something or not.

Brent rang Rick's cell phone and got his voice mail. He got the same on Rick's landline. Giving up, he headed for the shower.

* * *

At the office, Melinda told Brent there were no messages left from Rick. Only one from April Marsh. He trudged to his desk and dialed her.

"April, hello, Brent Marks, returning your call."

"Hello, Brent. Just checking in to find out where you are with the complaint."

"It's pretty much ready to go, but I'm waiting on something from my investigator. If he produces it, it could delay the filing by about a week."

"What is it?"

"I'm sorry, but I can't tell you about it now. It may not materialize at all, but if it does, it could help us quite a bit."

"You're the lawyer. Do you think it's at a point where I could review it, or do you still need to wait for your investigator for that?"

"Oh, sure, I can send you the draft. It's pretty complete. I'll send it to you by email."

Brent hung up, and continued to worry about Rick. He was an early riser, and it was already past 9 a.m.

"Mims, do I have any appointments this morning?"

"No, you're clear all day, why?"

"I'm going to head out to Penn's house. I'm getting worried about him."

* * *

Rick's car was parked in the driveway. That meant that he must have already been out and about and was preparing to go out again. Rick always left his car in the garage overnight. Brent rang the bell – no answer. He pounded on the door and called Rick's name. Still no answer. Brent let himself in with his copy of Rick's key.

"Rick! Dude, it's me, are you home?"

Again, no answer. Brent looked through every room of the small three bedroom house, but there was no sign of his friend anywhere. He decided to wait. If Rick's car was here, he could not be far behind.

* * *

After two hours of waiting, Brent decided to give up the ghost. He headed straight for the police station.

15

"It's not long enough to report a person missing," said the rookie desk cop at the Santa Barbara police station's public desk.

"Look, I'm a lawyer and I know the law. There's no time period for reporting a person missing under California law. And this guy is an ex-FBI agent."

"Then you should probably go to the FBI," said the clerk.

Brent managed to get the clerk to call a staff sergeant to take a report, and then he did head for the FBI's field office in Santa Barbara, as the clerk suggested.

The FBI's field office in Santa Barbara was an unimpressive, unmarked office in a plain wrap office building downtown. Brent rang the bell and an attractive young woman answered the door and invited him in. She introduced herself as Agent Angela Wollard.

"We do maintain a data base of missing persons, but unless it's a child and foul play is suspected, we don't really get actively involved in missing person's cases," said Agent Wollard.

"Not as interesting as pornography cases, I guess."

"Excuse me?"

Agent Wollard was obviously offended, and her finely manicured eyebrows frowned. Brent couldn't help thinking that he couldn't imagine a woman as attractive as her carrying a gun. She was about 30 years old, with light brown hair and eyes the color of sunlight shining through forest ferns. Not a formidable match for any street criminal at first glance, but quite intelligent.

"I'm sorry, that was uncalled for. This is different. Rick Penn is one of your own. He was…"

"Rick? He's missing?"

"You know him?"

"He was my training agent, my first day on the job."

That brought down the initial barriers, and Brent explained all the details. Wollard was quite thorough and exhaustive in her questioning; so much so that Brent became exhausted from it himself.

"This bank fraud case you're working on - can I take a look at it?" she asked.

"Well, it's not even filed yet, but I could give you a confidential draft of the complaint."

"Good, it may be helpful for background. Besides the current case, had he worked on anything recently where he had been threatened?"

"No, I'm the one who was threatened."

Brent explained the Joshua Banks case in detail.

Agent Wollard didn't believe in letting any lead go cold. Not only did she add Rick to the missing person's data base, she began working the case right away, starting with the last lead that Rick had been working in the case – Bernstein.

16

"I have to tell you, Agent Wollard, we were quite upset when we learned that your Mr. Penn had lied about being an FBI agent," said Bernstein, indignantly.

Bernstein leaned back in his seat, scratched his nose, ran his hand through his moustache and looked out the window toward downtown L.A. As she questioned him, she noted how ill at ease he seemed, and how he avoided eye contact with her. He was hiding something.

"Where were you yesterday, about 4 p.m., Mr. Bernstein?"

"I was working."

"What time did you leave the office?"

"I don't remember," he said, this time deliberately looking in her eyes.

"Would you mind if we checked with your office staff?"

"Am I under investigation?" he asked, raising his eyebrows and opening his mouth in shock.

"No."

"Well, then, I prefer that you didn't, because it could be embarrassing."

Angela couldn't go any further at this point, but she was uncomfortable with Bernstein's responses, and, at that point, he was the top suspect on her list if she should uncover any evidence of foul play.

* * *

The days droned on. It had already been three days since Rick was missing. Agent Wollard had recommended an investigator to fill in the gaps until Rick was found. But Brent's mind was heavy with the thought that Rick may never turn up, or worse, that he would turn up dead. And, to top it off he had trouble with his client.

"You haven't alleged murder as a predicate act," April exclaimed angrily, as she paced Brent's office.

"First of all, I would appreciate it if you would sit down," said Brent. April complied. There was nothing worse than having a fuming client bouncing against the walls of your office.

"Next, I have to tell you that I have been waiting for my investigator to come up with some new evidence on that very subject, but he's gone missing."

"What do you mean missing?"

"Missing. He was working the Bernstein angle when he just disappeared."

"It's Bernstein," she said. "I'm sorry about your investigator, but I know it's him."

"I don't, and that's why we can't just run out and file on a whim or a hunch."

"I understand that, but what more do you need?"

"It's called evidence, April. We discussed it before."

Her emotions were starting to grate on Brent, but the thought of Bernstein possibly murdering Rick gave him a pang of empathy for her.

"I told you, I'm the lawyer. That's a decision I will make."

"I know. I'm sorry."

"He's not just my investigator, April. He's also my best friend. And I can promise you, if Bernstein is guilty, he will fry."

Brent didn't like to react with emotion in front of a client. That was a bad choice, and it came inextricably intertwined with a promise, which was even worse. The fact was that he was sure that Bernstein was responsible for Rick's disappearance, but hope prevented him from fully realizing that it was too late to save him.

* * *

Brent found Agent Angela Wollard in her office, and he was a little irritated that she was not out in the field working on Rick's case. Now it was Brent who was acting like an emotional client.

"You seem a little angry, Mr. Marks."

"Brent, please."

"Brent."

"I know you've got other cases. I'm just upset and frustrated."

"Did you interview the investigator I suggested? He may be able to help."

"Not yet. I just want to ask you one thing."

"I can't discuss the details of the investigation, if that's what you want. Not at this stage."

"I know that. I just want to know if you think Bernstein is guilty."

"Wait a minute. I just said I can't…"

"I know, just give me the benefit of your gut feeling. He was your friend, too."

Angela leaned forward onto her desk, rested her cheek on her knuckles, and sighed. "I think he's hiding something."

17

It was day seven of Rick's disappearance. The air felt heavier, the light dimmer. Brent went through his morning routine, but nothing seemed right. Rick's absence had left a void in Brent that was now filled with a deep sadness. He knew that he would never see his friend again.

* * *

The investigator Angela had recommended seemed to be competent. A certified fraud examiner, Jack Ruder was also a retired FBI agent, from the Los Angeles office, about Rick's age, but it seemed he couldn't shake the old habit of always wearing a G-man style suit. Jack had intelligent brown eyes, a full head of brown hair, and that look that said "cop" all over himself. He had taken up the investigation where Rick had left off, and was able to put together a solid chain of evidence showing that the Marshes' loan had never been assigned to the mortgage backed securities trust, and the forged documents that Prudent Bank had used to try to assign it after the fact.

He had also put together a file of documents that proved that the Marshes had been promised a loan modification, but got a foreclosure instead. There was enough evidence of mortgage fraud to support any RICO complaint, but nothing to back up a murder allegation. Ruder had tried to interview Bernstein, but he had, of course, refused. The only chance Brent would have to interview him would be in his deposition.

The trouble with making an important decision was that you never had enough information to do it without hesitating. And it's the hesitation that gnawed at you and never helped you to make the decision. Brent decided to go with his gut feelings and added the predicate act of "murder" to the complaint.

***

The complaint was filed in downtown Los Angeles the next morning, and a press release on it went out right after filing. Brent didn't mention the word "murder" in the press release. RICO would be enough of an impact. By late afternoon, he had received a few email inquiries from journalists. The circus had begun.

Prudent Bank's agent for process was served with the summons and complaint immediately by a process server. But Brent had a special service in mind for Bernstein. Jack Ruder waited in his late model white Ford Crown Victoria outside Bernstein's house and waited for him to come home from work. At about 6:30 Bernstein pulled up in his new silver Mercedes Maclaren. Bernstein parked the Maclaren in his driveway, got out of it, and almost bumped into Jack, who handed him the summons and complaint.

"Steven Bernstein, I'm serving you with the summons and complaint in the case of Marsh v. Bernstein."

Bernstein's mouth gaped open. "Okay, you've served me, now get off my property," he spat.

"You may want to talk to me now, Mr. Bernstein."

"Fuck off. Talk to my lawyer."

"Oh, we will. You may want to get one with criminal defense experience. Have a good day."

Jack backed away from Bernstein, who stomped into his house, crumpling the complaint in his hand.

18

Litigation was war. A war that usually inflicted heavy casualties on both sides. It was an expensive and exhausting battle of wits. The rules of war for federal court were contained in the 86 rules of federal civil procedure, the rules of the local federal court, and the courtroom rules of the particular federal judge.

Everything had its time and place. The discovery rules were drafted to insure that there would be no surprises, and that each side had an opportunity to obtain the evidence that their opponent intended to present at trial. Brent prepared for a one year series of battles leading to the final one, which would be a trial by jury. He knew that the first series of battles would be a full assault on his complaint, to try to throw as much of it out of court as possible.

***

Brent prepared and filed a motion for preliminary injunction, to stay any foreclosure sale until the matter could come to a trial on the merits. To succeed on the motion, he had to show that the Marshes would be irreparably harmed if the foreclosure would be allowed to proceed without them having their day in court.

This would be fairly simple to prove. Mr. Marsh would stand to lose his only asset – his home. Each parcel of real estate was considered to be unique under the law. But Brent would also have to make a showing that he was likely to prevail when his case did come to trial. This was a tougher task.

He didn't have to actually prove his case. That would come at trial. What he had to do was to raise "serious questions" that tipped the balance of hardships more toward the Marshes than Prudent Bank. Brent's written motion took up every inch of the 25 page maximum he was allowed to file. Everything had to be put down on paper; oral argument on the motion in court was just for show; and to answer the judge's questions, if she had any.

She was Judge Virginia Masters, an ex-federal prosecutor, intimately familiar with the workings of the RICO law. Brent's opponents were the Goliath downtown Los Angeles firm of

Stein, Stewart and Rothstein, and Prudent Bank was their best client. They would fight tooth and nail to throw out Brent's case, with an unlimited litigation fund which allow for any expense. Brent was the "David" in this war; a one-man firm with a slingshot of an emotional case. If he could get it to the jury, he had a chance of winning.

The first assault launched by Stein, Stewart and Rothstein was by Joe Stein, one of the partners. It was the motion to dismiss that Brent had expected. He spent so many hours in legal research and fleshing out a brief in opposition to it that he lost all track of time. Minutes blended into hours, then into days and, before he knew it, he had been buried in his computer for an entire week. Brent knew he was nearing the end. And every time he thought he had come to the end, he knew it was good. It just had to be better.

"Boss, doesn't your cat ever get hungry?" asked Melinda, as she was leaving the office one day.

"Huh...what?" Brent looked up momentarily from the computer screen.

"Your cat. You do have a cat, right?"

"Yeah, what about her?"

"It's just that I always see you here, early in the morning, and you're here every afternoon when I go home. It seems like you're always in the office."

"Well, I have to get this done."

"I know boss, just saying. You want me to grab you something to eat?"

"Yeah, sure, that would be good," Brent said, not missing a keystroke.

"What do you want?"

"Huh?"

"To eat. What do you want to eat?"

"Oh, anything, anything."

19

The wood paneled courtroom on Spring Street held a full audience for the motion hearings on the Marsh case. Most of the audience consisted of journalists. Others were members of activists groups protesting mortgage fraud. April sat at the counsel table with Brent, anxiously waiting. Finally, Judge Virginia Masters entered the courtroom in her black robe, and climbed the stairs to her elevated perch. She strained her dark amber eyes through her 1960's style cat eye glasses at the assembly before her. She seemed impatient and unimpressed.

"Case Number CV 13 – 61940, Marsh vs. Prudent Bank. Counsel, please state your appearances," said Judge Virginia Masters, sternly, well aware of the media coverage, given her aspirations to loftier juristic heights. She had to appear to be strong to the entire public. "I'll hear argument on the motion to dismiss first."

Brent knew it was logical to decide the motion to dismiss first. If the case was dismissed, there would be no need to listen to argument on Brent's motion for an injunction to stop the foreclosure sale. Still, he hated to give Joe Stein the opportunity to take the podium first. He had a reputation for hogging the entire show, kind of like a Senate filibuster.

Joe Stein took the lectern, smiling for the press, as if he were trying to impress a jury that was not there. The grey haired devil looked smart and crisp in his three piece custom tailored suit, and he spoke with deliberate intonation – the mark of a great actor – as he fixed his steel grey eyes on the judge for his performance.

"Your Honor, the Plaintiff is attempting to capitalize on the wave of public sympathy surrounding foreclosures. Prudent Bank is not the Simon Legree of banking. Nobody wants to foreclose on the Marshes' house or any other house for that matter. But this is business and foreclosure is the last resort. In fact, Prudent Bank is proud of its track record of actually putting people into new homes, and..."

"Let me stop you right there, Mr. Stein," said Judge Masters. "We're not taping a commercial for Prudent Bank. The only person in this room you have to impress is me. So let's get on with it or I will exclude the press from the courtroom."

Judge Masters was a tough broad, with an overdose of testosterone, probably gained fighting the male adversaries she faced while trying cases for the U.S. Attorney's office. Brent had never appeared before her, and was already beginning to regret it.

"I'm sorry, Your Honor, I had only begun the introduction to my argument."

"Mr. Stein, you may think, with this battery of law clerks at my disposal, that I have not read each and every word of your motion and the opposition, as well as your reply to the opposition, but I can assure you that I have. This Court's time is precious, so please don't go over everything in your brief. Just emphasize the points that you have *not* covered in in the briefs."

"That goes for you, too, Mr. Marks," said the Judge.

Brent had felt a bolt of confidence at her bullying of Stein, until she came to that comment.

"Mr. Stein, I want you to speak to the issue of predicate acts for the RICO count," said Masters.

Not a good sign. That was the weakest link in Brent's case and she had zeroed in on it. Federal judges sometimes ask questions when they have already made up their mind about an issue, but want to seem to be fair to the opposition. Stein was beaming at the opportunity to go for the jugular vein in Brent's case.

"Your Honor, that is the weakest part of the Plaintiff's case," he argued. "The predicate act of murder…"

"Mr. Stein," said the Judge, interrupting him again, "let's discuss first the mail fraud and wire fraud allegations."

"Very well, Your Honor. In order to pass muster under Rule 9, allegations of fraud have to be specific. The four W's – "who what, when and where" – are missing here. These allegations fail under Rule 9 because they are generic against Prudent Bank. They also allege that documents were forged to cover up an alleged fraudulent scheme, but in cases of fraud, you have to show reliance. Nowhere is it alleged here that Mr. Marsh relied on the alleged forgeries and suffered damages because of that reliance. And they cannot prove that, Your Honor. That is why we are requesting that you dismiss this count with prejudice."

Brent felt like jumping up at this point, but protocol dictated that he keep his mouth shut until it was his turn to speak. Clients often interpreted following this protocol as a sign of weakness, but Brent had prepared April well.

"With regard to the bank fraud allegations, the Plaintiff has the same problem," Stein continued, in detail. "But the weakest link of all is the absurd allegation of murder."

Stein kept true to his reputation. His filibuster lasted for the entire ten minutes of his allotted argument time. It was clear, concise, and made sense. When Judge Masters signaled that the speech was over, Brent approached the podium, juiced with adrenalin.

"Your Honor, since, for the purposes of this motion, the allegations in the Plaintiff's complaint are to be taken as true, all we have to do is sufficiently *plead* an enterprise, which is Prudent Bank; and the conduct of that enterprise through a pattern of racketeering, or investment of a part of the income of the racketeering activity into Prudent Bank. This has all been alleged. To allege racketeering activity, we only to have plead two predicate acts.

"In the days leading to the demise of Tentane Mutual, Prudent Bank knew that it was going to take over the assets of Tentane during the FDIC seizure. In fact the seizure and the asset takeover happened almost simultaneously. When Prudent found out that many of its mortgages had not been assigned to the mortgage backed securities trust pool, that Tentane had parceled off and sold securities that were not backed by the mortgages, and that it had no right to collect or service those mortgages, it began an elaborate cover up, by forging notary signatures and recording documents more than three years after the fact.

"This is obtaining property owned by or under the control of a financial institution by means of false or fraudulent pretenses; one of the predicate acts. Prudent also utilized the U.S. mail to record the forged documents. This is the predicate act of mail fraud. Therefore the Plaintiff has pleaded a sufficient case under RICO."

"Mr. Marks," said the Judge. "Even if you do get past the hurdle of pleading fraud with specificity, which I am not sure that you do with the mail fraud issue, you still have the problem of reliance. Mr. Marsh already had his loan at the time of the alleged mail fraud and financial institution fraud. How could he have possibly relied on the alleged fraudulent actions three years after the fact?"

"Your Honor, with regard to financial institution fraud, we have alleged that Prudent Bank collected interest and principal from Mr. Marsh on his loan, and applied it to the MBS holders' accounts, even though the note and deed of trust were not properly transferred to the Trust. That collection is also based on the forgery and recordation of the assignment.

In fact, they had no true right to collect, and Mr. Marsh relied upon their representations that he was paying his mortgage payments to the correct loan servicer, when Adelay Gioriano, the employee of Prudent Bank, indicated to Mr. and Mrs. Marsh that the bank had taken over the loan and directed payment to be made to them."

"That still leaves you with the problem of the lack of specificity of the mail fraud allegation, Mr. Marks,"

"If Your Honor is not satisfied that we have alleged the mail fraud with certainty…"

"And I am not…"

"…Then I would point out to the Court the fact that the murder and attempted murder allegations also serves as predicate acts."

"You realize then, do you not, Mr. Marks, that your entire RICO case would depend upon proving a case of murder?"

"Or attempted murder, Your Honor. Yes, I do. There is no federal rule that says I have to plead murder with specificity."

"Your Honor, may I be heard please?" asked Stein.

"Are you finished, Mr. Marks?" asked the Judge.

"No, Your Honor, I am not. The Defendants have profited from the biggest bank default in history. The fraudulent and deliberately criminal acts committed by Prudent Bank and its predecessor nearly destroyed the entire world economy, and the government gave them billions of dollars in bailout money which they used, not to help people refinance, which they promised my client and countless others, but to foreclose on millions of homes and make obscene profits. The Plaintiff has sufficiently pleaded a case of racketeering and the motion to dismiss must be denied."

"Now we have the issue of standing," said the judge. "Your entire case, Mr. Marks, is predicated on the allegation that the Note and Deed of Trust are void because they were not transferred to the Trust Pool by the closing of the Pooling Service Agreement."

"That's right, Your Honor. Under *Glaski v. Bank of America,* the lack of assignment in conformance with the terms of the PSA renders the Note and Deed of Trust void."

"According to Mr. Stein's motion, your clients have no standing to enforce the terms of the PSA, and all the cases in this district agree with him. They are not parties to the PSA, nor are they third-party beneficiaries."

"That's true Your Honor, but the *Serrato* case recognizes that there are other ways to claim standing."

"I object, your Honor, *Serrato* is an unpublished case and Mr. Marks is citing non-binding dictum in the case."

"You'll get your chance on rebuttal, Mr. Stein, now please take your seat and let Mr. Marks finish."

"If the Note and Deed of Trust were left outstanding," said Brent, "it would subject Plaintiff to collection and foreclosure activities from multiple parties, thus causing injury to the Plaintiff, which gives rise to his standing to raise the issue, as a party injured by the contract, pursuant to Civil Code section 3412."

"That's a very clever argument, Mr. Marks. Mr. Stein, now it's your turn."

Brent left the podium feeling good. All through Stein's rebuttal, nothing had been said that could topple the strength of Brent's argument. That was the good news. The bad news was that, if he won the motion to dismiss, he would have to prove that an agent or employee of the bank murdered April's mother and tried to murder her father.

And, Brent could not assume he was out of the woods yet. The Judge took both the motion to dismiss and the motion for preliminary injunction under submission. She would render a written opinion on it in the week to come.

Brent could see from April's expression that she was very pleased. Stein did not appear so happy. He and his junior counsel walked out of the courtroom without saying good-bye and waded through the bevy of reporters outside the courthouse, treating them with a rapid-fire of "no comments."

Brent, on the other hand, could not wait to "bathe" in the sea of reporters. Before they exited, he said to April, "Now remember what I told you. Just let your expressions reveal your emotions, but let me do all the talking."

"Okay," she said, teary-eyed.

"Crying is okay, but let me talk about the case. We don't want Stein to claim we tainted the jury pool."

The jury pool was to be drawn from downtown Los Angeles and Brent could not be happier about that. He would try to pack the jury with people whose lives had been touched by foreclosure. All they had to do now was wait for the judge's decision and then the game was on.

20

Judge Masters rendered her decision on Friday, and it was a grand slam. She denied the motion to dismiss the complaint and granted an injunction to stay the foreclosure until trial. She also set a scheduling conference, which would mark the beginning of the parties' discovery. Brent had already prepared written requests for documents with the help of his new investigator, and a set of written questions, but the most sought after discovery tool was the deposition of Steven Bernstein. In the deposition, Brent could grill him under oath and find out what it would be like to have him on the witness stand at trial.

Brent met with Jack Ruder to plan a strategy for discovery of what essentially would be a murder case. April, at about the same time as Jack, was happy to have heard the good news that her case had not been thrown out. Brent introduced her to Jack as his new investigator.

"April, I have to tell you that what we've been through so far is nothing compared to what we will have to go through to complete this case," said Brent.

"I understand."

"Now, essentially what we have to do is to prove a murder case. And we have nothing to go on, so we're starting from square one. Jack, this is your case. Where do we begin?"

"Ms. Marsh, does your father ever communicate with you?"

"Never."

"Is he conscious, does he appear to be alert?"

"You know, he appears to be alert, but I just talk and talk, and he doesn't even seem to react to my presence."

"Well, if you're up for it, I want to bring in a friend of mine from my bureau days to talk to your father. She's a psychologist and has already reviewed your father's records."

"I suppose that would be alright, but I don't know what you're going to get out of it."

"We'd like to interview your father as soon as possible. Say, tomorrow afternoon?"

"Sure, that's fine."

Brent had convinced Angela to meet him for lunch at The Gallery Café right across from the Santa Barbara Art Museum. The Gallery Café was a small art gallery with a nice collection of paintings by local artists, but its finest attraction was not the art, but its beautiful stone paved courtyard, which was like a little grotto with vines and orchids climbing the rock walls. The chairs and tables were positioned around a three-tiered fountain, whose cascading water added another dimension to the dining experience. Angela was already seated at one when Brent walked in, and waved to her.

"Hello Angela," he said, smiling, as he took the seat opposite her.

"Hello Brent."

"I thought this would be a nicer way of meeting me than me always barging in on you, demanding information about Rick."

"I'm actually very glad that you did it," she said. "It's very pleasant."

"Me too, and since it's your lunch hour, I'm going to refrain from talking business so you can have a real lunch break. Just a little update before you go back to the office is all I ask."

"Well, we…"

"Angela, I do want to hear it, believe me I do, but I also mean what I said. What would you like for lunch?"

Angela was flattered and relaxed. Flattered because of the attention she was receiving from Brent and relaxed because it wasn't a "date." They tended to be too stressful; kind of like a job interview.

Brent watched Angela daintily sip her avocado cucumber gazpacho, as he tried his best not to make slurping sounds with his. Nothing was more unnerving to him than someone who ate with sound effects, like a Hollywood Foley artist.

"So what makes a nice girl like you join the FBI?" he asked, then suddenly realized that, in his eagerness to impress, he had come up with a cliché that sounded like a pick-up line. Angela graciously allowed him to sidestep it. She liked this rogue lawyer who showed no fear in facing down the "too big to fail" banks.

"Actually, I was going to be an attorney."

"Really?"

"Yes, really. Went to law school and everything. The guys at Quantico used to call me *Amicus Curiae.*

"You never tried the law? Never took the Bar?"

"No. I just got tired of seeing it being broken. So I decided to go after the bad guys."

Their conversation was interrupted by the Waiter, who set before them two fresh sea bass with potato puree and a French ratatouille.

"What about you Brent? What made you decide to go into law?"

"Instead of law enforcement? A healthy distrust for the police."

Brent was just kidding, of course, but he instantly worried that he may have offended her.

"All kidding aside, my dad recommended it. He said you can be your own boss, work anywhere you want, see the world."

"Sounds good."

"It has been, so far. Dad said he got up to the top stair of the law school, then changed his mind. Went into business school. Said it was the biggest mistake of his life."

Time passes by quickly, especially enjoyable time. Finally, it was Brent who looked at his watch. He had the afternoon interview of April's father at the convalescent home. As much as he wanted to stay, it was time to go back to work.

"Angela, I'm glad we did this, but I'm afraid it's time for me to get to work."

"Me too, actually."

"Just let me ask you, is there any hope for a break in Rick's investigation?"

"Nothing earthshattering yet, unfortunately."

"Anything; something miniscule maybe?"

"Well, we did find something strange. We never found Rick, or any of his personal effects. But we did search the hard drive on his Mac and we found that it had been accessed from a remote location and all the data wiped clean."

"Rick would never erase his hard drive."

"That's what I thought. We're trying to recover anything we can from it."

***

On the way to the convalescent home, Brent's mind was occupied. Then he saw them. The same two goons in the white Mustang that had followed him from the Sheriff's Office were again on his tail. This time, he turned around immediately, made his way back to Angela's office, and parked in front of the building. Luckily, Angela was just coming in. Brent got out and waved to her. The goons sat tight in their car.

"Those are the same two guys who followed me right before Rick went missing," he told her.

"They could have something to do with the case. Wait in your car until I call you. I'll get my car and follow behind them."

"I'm headed to the rest home to interview April's father, and I really don't want them following me there."

"Okay, I'll get SBPD to pull them over for a traffic offense or something, and then interrogate them. I just want to get behind them long enough to establish that they really are following you."

Brent did as he was told, pulling out after he received Angela's call. The goons pulled out after him, as expected, but he didn't see Angela's car anywhere. Obviously, she was better at her job than they were.

As Brent passed La Cumbre Road, about halfway to the Oakview Extended Care Home, he saw a pair of red lights pop on behind the goons' car. They pulled to the side almost immediately.

21

George Marsh was a shadow of his former self. Once a tall, strong, rock of a man, he was now broken and frail. With a thin veil of skin stretched over his skull, it looked like the Angel of Death had already come to call on him. April was sitting next to his bed, holding his hand, as if she were sitting a vigil.

Jack Ruder, dressed in a two piece gray suit as always, and looking very FBI-like, had brought Dr. Beverly Senlon, a middle aged woman, with light brown hair, eyes the brown of fine cognac, and a pleasant plump face with rosy cheeks. She looked very calm and friendly, and was wearing a two piece mustard yellow skirt suit. She had, apparently, formulated her personal style in the 90's and her fashion remained stuck in time.

"Talk to your father, dear – introduce him to us," said Senlon to April.

April hesitated. "Go ahead, dear," said Senlon.

"Dad, I've brought some people here who are going to help us," said April. "This is our lawyer, Brent Marks. He's taking our case against the bank. And this is Jack Ruder, our investigator, and Dr. Senlon, who is going to help you talk to us."

George Marsh's face remained fixed, his mouth drooped open, and his eyes stared into a point in time that nobody else knew. Maybe not even him.

"Now, dear, your father is still very much with us. We know that because there is plenty of brain activity showing up on his CAT scans. We just have to figure out how to get through to him wherever he is."

"What do you mean?" she asked.

"Because of the brain damage, he may not be perceiving his environment the same way we do. We've hooked up to this machine to measure his vital signs, which could help us know if he's trying to communicate with us, so we're going to try to get through, okay?"

"Okay."

Dr. Senlon shined a small penlight into each of George Marsh's eyes. His pupils reacted to the light.

"Now, Mr. Marsh, I know you can see me because your eyes are working just fine," said Senlon. She clipped her penlight onto her pocket. "Can you hear me?" She clapped her hands loudly and Marsh blinked.

"Very good, Mr. Marsh. It looks like you can hear me too. Blink your eyes if you can hear me."

George Marsh did not blink, and just kept staring into space.

"It's hopeless," said April. "I told you, I've tried so many times to talk to him."

"Now, now, dear. We don't give up that easily. Mr. Marsh, this is my friend, Jack Ruder. He's going to talk to you about Prudent Bank."

"Mr. Marsh," said Jack, "Do you remember Steven Bernstein from Prudent Bank?"

Marsh showed no reaction at all. Jack held up an 8x10 photograph of Bernstein. "Do you know this man?" he asked.

Just then, Marsh's monitor began beeping, as his heart rate increased from 80 bpm to 130 bpm, and his breath came in pants.

"I think we have something," said Senlon. "Mr. Marsh, do you know who this man is in the picture?"

Marsh's heart rate continued to rise, as did his blood pressure.

"We have a reaction," said Senlon. Don't worry, Mr. Marsh, your daughter is safe. Mr. Ruder here used to work for the FBI. She's in very good hands. But we need your help."

A single tear streaked down George Marsh's left cheek.

22

The discovery phase of litigation was the most boring, and, of course, Brent's least favorite. Discovery methods included requests for admissions, which were used to ask the opposing parties to admit that a fact was true, interrogatories, which allowed you to pose written questions to them, and requests for production of documents and physical evidence.

The entire process reminded him of the cartoons where one character would throw in his line, and the fish would take the bait off, replace it with an old boot or tire, then tug on the line to make the fisherman think he had caught something. Responses to written discovery were inevitably filled with objections rather than information.

The most effective tool in discovery was the deposition, which allowed a lawyer to actually question a witness under oath, in the presence of a court reporter. Even if the witness was lying, you could still get a good look at his or her demeanor, and it was a good indication of how his or her testimony would play out in front of a judge or jury. Jack Ruder had been helpful in gathering evidence in the form of documents, which aided Brent in identifying witnesses and streamlined the written discovery process. At this point, Brent had exhausted all forms of written inquiry over the past two months, and it was now time to conduct depositions. First in line was the deposition of Steven Bernstein.

**

The small conference room in Brent's office, which was usually empty, was now brimming with activity. The court reporter had set up her recording equipment, and the videographer had set up his video camera. A wire with a small lapel microphone had been set out on the table in front of every seat. The only thing that was missing was Steven Bernstein, his personal lawyer, and the lawyer from Stein, Stewart and Rothstein.

Jack Ruder had already come and gone. He had a very small role in the deposition process, but it was a very important one. Bernstein's seat was right next to the court reporter, so she could take down every word that he said, and right across from the videographer's camera. It was a high backed leather chair; the kind that Bernstein had in his own office. But the point of having such a chair was not so Bernstein would be comfortable.

Normally, Brent would want him to be as uncomfortable as possible. Ruder had cleaned and outfitted the back of the chair with the smallest of electrical charges, designed to pick up any loose hairs, which would stick to the chair like iron fibers to a magnet. Ruder would come during the lunch break and after the deposition was over to sweep the chair back with an adhesive roller, to see if he could pick up any hair samples that could be used for DNA comparison with the hair fibers found at the Marsh crime scene. Since this was not a criminal case, Brent didn't have to worry about violating Bernstein's civil rights. April sat on Brent's side of the table. Her job would be to keep her eyes trained on Bernstein as an intimidation tactic. It was an unpleasant role for her, but her disdain for Bernstein gave her the power to fulfill it.

Bernstein walked in with his personal lawyer, William Black, who sat on the left side of him, and John Reiser, the junior lawyer from Stein, Stewart and Rothstein took up the other space next to him. Black looked to be in his 50's, dressed in the traditional lawyer uniform – a two piece light brown suit. The junior looked about 35, and wore the same uniform.

Brent could be sure that they had both skillfully prepared Bernstein to keep him from answering any questions they did not want him to answer. But those types of questions were very limited. Brent had to tread rather carefully. If he pushed him too far, Bernstein could "take the Fifth;" claim his Fifth Amendment privilege against self-incrimination; and refuse to answer any question that could implicate him in the murder of April's mother and the attack against her father.

Bernstein leaned back into the tall chair, looking smug, moustache twitching. He had, no doubt, been through mock depositions with his lawyers, and was prepared for the scrutinous eye of the video camera. After giving a set of dry and boring instructions, and going through a huge set of equally boring documents to set a foundation, Brent embarked on a hunt to capture his prey. He went for shock value.

"Mr. Bernstein," said Brent, having placed several graphic photographs of April's murdered mother before him, "You do recognize this woman, don't you?"

April glared at Bernstein with burning eyes, as Bernstein avoided the photograph.

"Not really, no."

"Come on, Mr. Bernstein, you know that this is Elena Marsh, isn't that correct?"

"I can't really say."

"Mr. Bernstein, where were you on the night of November 25, 2008, from about 12 midnight through 3 a.m.?"

"I don't remember."

"Isn't it true that you were at the Marshes' home in Hope Ranch on November 25th, Mr. Bernstein?"

April's face expressed disbelief. She continued her stare down.

"No."

"Let me go back in time, a bit, Mr. Bernstein," said Brent. "Mr. and Mrs. Marsh were customers of Tentane Mutual, isn't that correct?"

"Yes, they were."

"And, in August 2006, you recommended a loan product to them, is that correct?"

"Yes."

"Mr. Bernstein, this loan product had an initial interest rate lower than the prime rate at the time, isn't that true?"

"Yes."

"And it had an adjustable rate rider allowing the interest rate to adjust every year, isn't that also true?"

"Yes, it did."

"Mr. Bernstein, I'm showing you a copy of the note and deed of trust. Take a minute to look it over please."

Bernstein leafed through the copy. "Yes?"

"Does that look like the loan you sold them?"

"It looks like it could be, yes."

"And isn't it true that Mr. Marsh was worried that he wouldn't be able to make the payments in the event of an interest rate increase."

"That was a concern of his."

"And he was qualified for the loan based on the initial payments, correct?"

"Yes."

"Isn't it true, Mr. Bernstein that, in June 2007, the mortgage payments increased to $8,500 per month, as set forth in the tables in front of you, marked as Exhibit 34?"

"That looks about right."

"Mr. Bernstein, isn't it also true that, given Mr. Marsh's income when the loan was initialized, he would have *not* qualified for payments of $8,500 per month?"

"Objection, irrelevant," barked John Reiser.

"You can answer the question, Mr. Bernstein," said Brent. "There's no judge here."

"I don't know if he would have qualified or not," said Bernstein.

"Don't lie, Mr. Bernstein…"

"Objection argumentative," said Black.

"Join," said Reiser.

"The tables we've identified as Exhibit 31 were used by you to do rough qualifying, isn't that true?"

"Yes."

"And based on Mr. Marsh's income in Exhibit 26, there is no way he would qualify for the increased payment, isn't that true?"

"He was hoping for an increase in his business," said Bernstein.

"Mr. Bernstein, you know that is not true…"

"Objection, argumentative!" said Black.

"Join!"

"You knew that George Marsh's business was in the dumps, didn't you?"

"Objection!" said Reiser.

"It wasn't doing that well," said Bernstein.

"He told you that was why he needed the loan, isn't that true?"

"That was one of the reasons."

"And you told him not to worry about the increases in interest rates, didn't you Mr.

Bernstein?" asked Brent, raising his voice an octave.

"I don't remember."

"Of course you remember, Mr. Bernstein," said Brent, raising his voice even higher. "In fact, you told Mr. Marsh not to worry about increases because you would just refinance the mortgage for him, isn't that true?"

"I don't recall. We may have mentioned some refinancing opportunities down the road."

"Of course you did, Mr. Bernstein."

"Objection, argumentative and asked and answered," said Reiser. "Counsel, are you going to continue this line of questioning?"

"Of course I am, Mr. Reiser, don't interrupt me. Mr. Bernstein, you told Mr. and Mrs. Marsh not to worry about rate increases because they could always refinance, isn't that true?"

"Like I said, I don't recall."

"Maybe this will refresh your recollection," said Brent, throwing down a new exhibit. "This is a sworn statement given by Mr. Marsh that, at the time of signing, he initially refused to sign and that you convinced him to sign by telling him that you could always refinance the loan to avoid higher payments, isn't that correct?"

"I don't recall."

"You also said, and I quote, 'Don't worry about an increase in payments. Let's get you into this loan, and you can always get into a non-qualifying loan in the next 18 months because your house is going to be increasing in value.' Didn't you say that to Mr. and Mrs. Marsh?"

"Objection," said Black. "The witness has already testified that he doesn't recall."

"And I'm refreshing his recollection. Didn't you say that to Mr. and Mrs. Marsh?"

"I may have said something like that, but I don't remember exactly."

Brent spent the morning grilling Bernstein on everything from A through Z on the Prudent Bank takeover of Tentane Mutual, including their late assignment of the Marsh deed of trust into the trust pool and the subsequent cover up.

* * *

After the break, Brent set up Bernstein for the real torture.

"Mr. Bernstein, in October 2008, you discovered, did you not, that Prudent Bank was under investigation by the FBI and a federal grand jury for alleged bank fraud, isn't that correct?"

"Yes, I did."

"And did you come to learn that the FBI had spoken to Mr. and Mrs. Marsh in connection with that investigation?"

"I don't recall."

"Come on, Mr. Bernstein, you knew that Mr. Marsh had made a complaint to the FBI about the way his loan refinance application was handled."

"I recall something about that, yes."

"And you spoke to Mr. Marsh about his complaint, isn't that correct?"

"I wanted to see if there was anything I could do to help him."

"Mr. Bernstein, because Mr. and Mrs. Marsh were going to expose the illegal transfer of their loan   to Prudent Bank, you stood to lose your promotion to Vice President, isn't that correct?"

Bernstein clutched the armrests of the chair so tightly his knuckles turned three different shades.

"No!"

"Yes, Mr. Bernstein! Yes! And when you found out about what Mr. and Mrs. Marsh intended to tell the Grand Jury, you went to their house on November 25th…"

"No!"

"Let me finish! You went to their house on November 25th…"

"No I didn't!"

"And you killed Mrs. Marsh..."

April continued to look at Bernstein, although the sight of him made her sick. She couldn't take much more of him.

"Objection!" said Black.

"Join!" said Reiser.

"No!"

"And you left only after you thought you had also killed Mr. Marsh..."

"No!"

"Counsel, I object to this line of questioning," yelled Black.

"I'm not finished! You bashed Mrs. Marsh's head in, didn't you Mr. Bernstein?" demanded Brent. "And the last time you saw her, she looked like THIS!" said Brent, throwing the gruesome photo in front of him."

April covered her eyes with her hand and turned away. Bernstein shot up from his chair, ripping the lapel microphone from his jacket and throwing it against the table. "I don't have to listen to this shit!" he said.

"On the contrary, Mr. Bernstein, you *do* have to listen to this shit. Sit down, I haven't excused you." Ignoring Brent, Bernstein stormed out of the conference room.

"Let the record show that Mr. Bernstein has refused to answer the last question and has left the room while still on the record," said Brent.

Both lawyers stood up and Reiser said, "We need a conference with Mr. Bernstein, can we go off the record?"

"Well, it's a little late for that," said Brent.

"And lay off the theatrics, or we'll have to move for sanctions," said Black.

"Do what you have to do," said Brent, as Reiser and Black stormed out of the room. "But be back in five minutes so we can finish this today. Otherwise be prepared to come back tomorrow morning."

Jack came in to sweep the chair with the roller. After a few minutes, he exclaimed, "We have a hair!"

23

FBI Agent Angela Wollard was frustrated by the lack of leads in the Rick Penn missing person's case. She had exhausted all the usual inquiries; interviewed all family members, friends, and acquaintances. Rick had simply vanished from the face of the earth.

His blue Porsche Boxster had been left in the driveway of his abandoned home, and a thorough sweep by the crime lab had uncovered no physical evidence to indicate "foul play" with the exception of one thing, which was not evidence at all. Penn's car had been wiped clean. There was not a solitary fingerprint on it, which was very odd. Someone had gone to the trouble of making sure that the car had no stories to tell. Certainly Penn's own fingerprints should have been all over the door handle and steering wheel, but they were not. It was as if the car had been driven there by a ghost. All of her experience and all of her instincts led Angela to the insight that this lack of evidence of criminal activity was more of a cover up than a coincidence.

It was this nagging thought that drove Angela out to Rick's house on a quest for that epiphany that would put her on the trail for whom she was sure was Rick's murderer. Rick's care had been left where it was. Since there was no crime scene, there was no reason to impound it.

She saw it as she approached and parked, and stared at it for several moments before she exited her own vehicle, carrying her evidence kit, and slipped on her gloves for that hopeful evidentiary discovery she was about to make.

Approaching the car, she actually talked to it. "Okay, time to tell me where you came from and who drove you here."

She felt a bit foolish, as the best evidence team in the FBI had already been over the car thoroughly, but the Colombo in her could not let it go, so she started with the outside of the car, scraping soil samples from the inside of the tire treads, the undercarriage, the bumpers, and even squashed bugs from the headlights. Then she opened the car with the bump key from the evidence envelope and went over the entire interior, vacuuming the carpet and upholstery for hairs and fibers, and dusting the dashboard, doors and seats for prints.

After what seemed like hours, Angela realized that she was exhausted, as well as hungry, and, upon her final assessment, figured that she had kicked the dead horse enough times. She decided to fuel up at lunch, then head back to the lab to deposit her findings for examination.

* * *

When she arrived at the office, Brent Marks was sitting in the waiting room.

"Hi Brent. Don't give me any business about working the Rick Penn case. I've been at it all day."

"Hey, calm down. Did you ever consider I may just be dropping by to take you to lunch?"

"Right. Well, you're too late for that. Anyway, I decided to go out to the car and give it the once-over again."

"Why? I thought it was clean."

"Maybe too clean. It's been wiped clean, in fact."

"Interesting. So did you find anything on your second sweep?"

"Don't know yet. Have to drop by the lab to put it in for analysis. By the way, did you get those results back on the hair that you got from the deposition?"

"Yes. Unfortunately, it didn't match the hair at the crime scene. But I know he's guilty. Probably of the Marsh murder and Rick's."

"We don't know that Rick was murdered."

"Come on, Angela. Do you think my best friend would just disappear without letting me know? And in the middle of a case this big?"

"Look, nobody takes this case more seriously than I do. That's why I went over the car again myself."

"I know. I'm sorry. I just can't believe he's not here anymore. You don't know how many times I've been working on something on this case and go to dial his number to ask him a question, and then I realize he's not going to be there. The other day I was thinking about what to get him for his upcoming birthday. And, until I know what really happened, there's still that hope that he might still be alive."

Angela put her hand on Brent's and said, reassuringly, "We'll find him."

24

Beverly Senlon was in the waiting room in Brent's office when he arrived, leafing through one of Melinda's old People magazines.

"Hello, Dr. Senlon," said Brent. "Come in," and gestured toward his office.

Senlon came into Brent's office, sat down and opened her briefcase. From it, she withdrew a small manila file folder.

"So, how is it going with Mr. Marsh?"

"We've actually made a great deal of progress," said Senlon, who smiled as she put on her reading glasses and opened the folder. "Our tests show that Mr. Marsh is fully aware of what is going on in his surroundings and that he hears and understands us. The problem is that he cannot communicate with us, because of his injuries – that is – in any traditional way."

"What does that mean?"

"Mr. Marsh was severely injured in the attack. He suffered traumatic injuries to his brain and spinal cord, which have left him completely paralyzed and unable to move or speak, use sign language, or to point at a spelling board. But we are using methods called augmentative and alternative communication, or AAC, to try to establish a method of communication."

"Do you think he may be able to testify in court using this alternative communication?"

"That is our ultimate goal. We're formulating a picture board with special symbols that he will point to by his eye movements."

"That sounds complicated."

"Yes and no. It's kind of like learning another language. Mr. Marsh is in kindergarten now."

"When will he be in high school?"

"He's a very intelligent and capable man, Mr. Marks, but it's going to take some time. He gets frustrated at times. Imagine having something to say but not being able to say it? But we will get there."

"How do you know that?"

"Instinct and experience. He's trying very hard, because he has something very important to tell us. We just don't know what it is yet."

***

"Jack, we're getting down to the wire and I didn't get much in discovery on mail fraud. What have you got for me?" Brent leaned on his elbows on the desk as Jack ruffled through his files.

"Not much."

"Come on, Jack, do you really want me to prove up a murder case to get my RICO? We're hanging on a thread here."

"I know, I know. The subpoenas have been served on the notaries, so we have them on the robo-signing."

"I can depose them. What else?"

"I ran down all the leads on the internal mailing records. It's just that, unless it's certified, we can't really prove that they used the postal service."

"Let's get as close as we can. I can zero in on their standard practices using the mail with the notaries. Just try to pin down a mail clerk or someone. With a multi-state operation like Tentane's was, it can't be that difficult."

"Okay."

"And remember, discovery cutoff is in two months. We have to jam on this, Jack."

***

Einstein said time is an illusion. Tell that to a lawyer preparing a federal case. One thing was for sure – you can procrastinate, but time will not – and you will run out of it soon enough. Brent knew only too well that he would never have enough time to prepare. There was just the time he had and that was it. Whether he was ready or not, he had to be ready.

25

Angela could not believe her eyes as she opened the envelope with the test results. From vacuuming Penn's car, not only had she picked up a hair fiber, but it also matched the hair found at the Marsh crime scene. She had run the comparison on a hunch, and the hunch had paid off. Penn's disappearance was definitely connected to the Marsh murder. She called ahead to Brent and headed out in the direction of his office to share the news.

Everyone had given up on George Marsh. They assumed that, since he didn't appear to have a reaction that they recognized as communication, he was a vegetable. George Marsh was a prisoner of his own body. With no ability to speak or to move anything except his eyes, he had long since given up on life. But if he could just help his daughter; protect her; that was worth any effort.

Dr. Senlon seemed to know what she was doing, but Marsh was frustrated. He had something very important to tell April, but no capacity to compose it without speech. If he could have moved his arms, he would have grabbed that stupid symbol board and thrown it to the ground.

"You're doing very well, Mr. Marsh. Let's review the new symbols we learned today," said Dr. Senlon, as April looked on. "April, this will eventually help you to communicate with your father."

The communication board had numbers 0 through 10 and the alphabet, surrounded by common phrases, including "yes" and "no." It also had the days of the week and the months of the year on the bottom of the board.

Finally, Senlon decided to try an experiment. "Mr. Marsh," she asked, "are you ready to talk to me about what happened the night your wife was murdered?" she asked.

Marsh blinked once, indicating yes.

"Very good!" said Senlon, and she proceeded to take Marsh through the complicated process of telling his story with the board, using Senlon as his interpreter. At the end, April looked at her with curious eyes. Senlon smiled.

"We have a witness," she said.

* * *

Angela had found a break in the case, but all it proved was that the same unknown person who had been in the Marshes' house sometime before or during the murder had also been, at one time, either a passenger or driver of Rick Penn's car. All eyes were on Angela as she revealed the contents of the report.

"I don't have the authority to release it to you as part of the Penn case, but if you subpoena reports of any physical evidence connected with your RICO case against the bank, I'm sure that the FBI will release it to you," said Angela.

Jack and Angela could see that Brent was deep in the invisible labor of thought. Finally, he said, "We're no better off than we were before. Jack, you need to get me something. Put a face to this hair sample."

"I'm on it."

"And Angela, thank you so much for this. I know you're treading on dangerous ground revealing it to us."

"I just want to get this guy," she said.

"As do we all. We have more good news. Dr. Senlon had a breakthrough with George Marsh, so I'm putting him on the witness list. So far, her report says that Marsh and his wife were attacked by two men, and he can identify them both. She also says that there was a third guy at the house, calling the shots, but she couldn't nail anything down on him. Senlon and Jack are going to go over some mug shots with him tomorrow."

"Make sure you show him a picture of Bernstein," said Angela.

"Is that another hunch, Agent Wollard?"

"Call it an educated guess," she replied.

"You heard the lady, Jack. And if that doesn't work, get a sketch artist over to the rest home. We're still light years away from proving murder, even under a civil standard. We all know what we need to do."

26

The deposition of George Marsh could go only one of two ways – success or disaster. If a success, Brent would be able to present his entire testimony – live– at the trial. If a disaster, anything that was not answered by Marsh in the deposition would not be allowed into evidence during his testimony.

Brent was breaking new ground in presenting a witness by means of augmentative and alternative communication. There was no case law that he found that could support it. On the other hand, that also meant that there was no case law against it.

The bank would challenge George Marsh's competency to testify and the judge, not the jury, would be the one who would decide whether to allow his testimony by means of AAC or not. So there were two hurdles to jump through to get Marsh's testimony before the jury at trial.

Brent had little time to prepare Marsh, because he didn't want to wear him out for the ordeal that lay ahead, so he had gone through the basics, mostly to establish a rhythm with Dr. Senlon, who would be interpreting Marsh's communications.

George Marsh was strapped in a wheelchair equipped with a neck brace next to the court reporter. Dr. Senlon sat in a chair by his side, dressed in a smart, crisp suit, looking very doctorly.

After they had settled in, Bill Black showed up with Bernstein. Black, Bernstein's personal lawyer, was a rough and tumble litigator with 30 years behind his belt. True to his name, he wore a jet black suit with a dark blue shirt and a purple tie, which accentuated the blue rays in his hazel eyes. Bernstein trained his eyes on Marsh as he took a seat. He looked like he was searching for some kind of reaction. Five minutes later, Joe Stein himself took his place at the conference table. Stein stole the spotlight immediately.

"Counsel, before we go on the record, I would like to make it perfectly clear that if this deposition is handled the same way as the Bernstein deposition, not only will we seek sanctions, but we will also be making a complaint to the Bar for unethical conduct."

"Let's go on the record," Brent said to the Court Reporter. "Please Mr. Stein, tell me what you just told me."

"I'm not a witness here," said Stein.

"Oh, but you are. You just threatened me."

"Counsel, I merely reminded you of your ethical obligations and that you would be held to answer to any unethical conduct."

"And may I remind you, Mr. Stein, that this may be your deposition, but any pressuring of this witness will result in my seeking sanctions."

"Please swear in Mr. Marsh and Dr. Senlon," Brent said to the court reporter. "Mr. Marsh," said Stein, ignoring Brent, "Can you please state your name for the record?"

Senlon began pointing to symbols on the symbol board and stated, "George," and then, "Marsh. My name is George Marsh."

"Excuse me, Madame, but Mr. Marsh must speak for himself," said Stein.

"He is speaking for himself," said Brent. You knew full well that we are using Dr. Senlon for augmentative and alternative communication. You have a copy of her CV right here."

"That is something that will never pass in court, especially after my motion in limine," snorted Stein.

"You can make whatever motions you want, Mr. Stein, but there being no judge for this deposition, I suggest you continue your questioning."

The deposition went on for a grueling two hours until Brent requested a recess. Each answer took an incredibly long time for Marsh to answer, and Stein had not even finished the preliminaries. Brent saw that Stein's main objective was to break Marsh down.

"Mr. Marsh needs a break."

"If we break every two hours, we'll never get done at this pace," said Stein.

"Off the record," said Brent, and Senlon wheeled Marsh out.

"Marks, do you really want to torture this old man?" asked Stein.

"You're the one torturing him."

"You know what I mean. The judge is never going to allow this. You think I like making hamburger out of this poor guy for no reason?"

"Grind away, Mr. Stein. Mr. Marsh is not a well man. His testimony needs to be preserved. The federal rules give you seven hours with him. At that point, I'm going to have my direct with him."

Stein ran the marathon with Marsh, exhausting him physically and mentally. What made it even more difficult was that everything seemed to be in slow motion. Marsh had to listen to the question, and then Senlon had to interpret the answer, which took the longest amount of time. The process must have been most frustrating for Marsh, who had a story to tell, but was limited by the means. Throughout the ordeal, Bernstein kept his intimidating eyes trained on Marsh. Thankfully, Stein ran through his communications with Bernstein, who proposed the loan, and identified Marsh's loan application, which was made out in Bernstein's handwriting. Finally, on the last minute of the last hour, Stein, although not finished, was obliged to turn over the witness to Brent, but at that time, Marsh was exhausted and his brain was nothing but Swiss cheese.

"Mr. Marsh, Exhibit A is your loan application – is this in your handwriting?"

Marsh indicated to Senlon and Senlon said, "No."

"Did you see who wrote this application?"

"Yes."

"Who was it?"

"Mr. Bernstein."

"Was it done in his office?"

"Yes. I brought my papers to his office, he made the application and I signed it."

"Did you propose that Mr. Bernstein help you with a loan on your home?"

"No, Mr. Bernstein proposed it."

"What did he say he could do for you in terms of making a loan?"

"Objection," said Black. "Hearsay."

"You can answer, Mr. Marsh."

Marsh looked at Bernstein, who regarded him with a cold, dead stare.

"He said that we could get into a sub-prime loan, but not to worry, because the property value was strong enough to refinance it in 24 months."

"And were you able to refinance in 24 months?"

"No. Mr. Bernstein said we didn't qualify and that we would have to be delinquent in our payments to apply for a loan modification instead of a refinance."

"And did you stop making payments?"

"Yes."

"Why?"

"Because it was the only way to get a lower monthly payment."

"Mr. Marsh, I'm going to show you a document and ask if you can identify it."

Dr. Senlon held the papers for Mr. Marsh to slowly read, then he indicated, "This looks like the loan modification request."

"And what was the result of that request?"

"It was denied."

"After the denial of your loan modification, did you resume making payments?"

"Yes, but we were always behind."

"Mr. Marsh, do you remember getting a letter from Prudent Bank in September 2008, telling you where to send your new payments?"

"Yes."

"Does this look like the letter?" asked Brent, holding it up for Marsh to read.

"Yes."

"And who did you understand your lender would be after this letter?"

"Prudent Bank."

"So, in reliance on this letter, you made your monthly payments to Prudent Bank."

"Objection," said Stein.

"Correct," said Senlon.

"Mr. Marsh, do you remember the night of November 25, 2008?"

Marsh's eyes started to twitch, and tears welled up in them.

"Yes."

"Tell me what you remember about that night when you and your wife were attacked."

"There were three of them who came at me," said Marsh. "They were all wearing masks, but I was able to pull one off right before I was knocked out."

"Did you recognize the man whose mask you pulled off?"

Marsh's eyes began to twitch again, and tears flowed down his cheeks.

"It was you!" he exclaimed.

"Who?"

"It was you!"

"I wasn't sure at first, but now I'm positive it was you."

The tears continued to flow down Marsh's cheeks and he began to cough and sputter, like a boiled over coffee pot.

"I think he needs a break," said Senlon.

"Mr. Marks, your time is up anyway," said Stein.

"But I'm not finished."

"Yes, you are. This is my deposition and the seven hours are up. I will not stipulate to more. Off the record please, Ms. Court Reporter."

Stein, Bernstein and Black got up in unison and walked out of the conference room.

"Stay on the record please, these gentlemen are still here. I am going to move for a protective order to continue this deposition. The motion will be filed tomorrow."

"File what you wish," said Stein, as the three left Brent's office.

27

Brent left the office around 2 a.m., after having finished the motion and filing it electronically. The nagging grief that was always on his mind since Rick Penn went missing was like a horrible weight on his head – a weight he had to drag around every day. He had been ignoring the pangs of hunger from his stomach until his body was too tired to pay attention to them anymore. When he had finally caught himself reading the same passage over and over again in the same case, he had decided to call it quits and go home to get some sleep.

Brent exited the office, laptop slung over his shoulder, and fished in his pocket for the keys to lock up. Suddenly, he was slammed up against the wall, face first, like he had been hit by a truck. He tried to turn and look at his attacker, but two strong gloved hands grabbed his head and smashed it into the wall. Then he was bailed through the doorway, like a baggage handler would throw a suitcase. When Brent was brave enough to raise his head, he saw two men in ski masks, who began to kick him and stomp on him, as if they were trying to kill a snake. Then, the lights went out.

When Brent came to, he felt the pain that so permeated his body, it was impossible for him to assess his injuries. He surveyed the office as best he could under the circumstances. His laptop was gone, as was Melinda's computer, and file folders and their spilled contents wallpapered the floor in a kind of collage of yellow and white paper. The file cabinets were all open and askew.

Brent tried to get up, but only got as far as his knees, which screamed in pain, and he fell back to the floor. He crawled to Melinda's desk, and climbed up the leg of it. As he reached the top, searing pains shot through his right rib cage. He reached the phone, dialed 911, and then passed out again.

***

As objects were coming into focus in Brent's hospital room, a few blocks away, in Sunny Acres Assisted Living Home, two shadows slipped into the room of George Marsh.

It was like the creepiest nightmare – hearing something in the room – but not being able to scream. As the two dark figures came into view, a surge of adrenalin rushed through George Marsh's arteries. He tried to run, but he could not get up. His eyes recoiled in terror as one masked figure raised his ski mask over his forehead, his lips stretched over his yellow teeth. And George Marsh pissed himself.

"It's us, old man," said the thug. "We've come to finish the job."

George's eyes wildly scanned the room, looking for help. He tried to scream, he tried to run, but it was no use. His brain commanded, but the body could not obey. The dark shadow of the pillow was the last thing George Marsh saw, as it was pushed against his face, taking the last bit of life he had.

28

To Jack, Brent appeared to be babbling, as he attempted to speak through the pain killers.

"Don't try to speak, buddy," he said.

"Not safe," said Brent.

"You're safe, you're safe– everything will be alright."

"No, no, no, not safe!" Brent struggled to form the words with his dry, broken swollen lips.

"Just try to calm down, you've been beat up really bad."

A male doctor in a white gown entered the room with a nurse. "Ah, Mr. Marks. You're up," he said.

"Not… not safe. George not safe."

"Don't try to speak, Mr. Marks. Just relax," said the doctor. "When you're ready to talk, there are some gentlemen from the police department who want to talk to you."

Brent, animated, tried to scream. "Not safe. George not safe...tell...police!"

Suddenly, Jack realized what Brent was trying to say. "I've got it, we'll make sure he has round the clock protection," he said, and he quickly left the room.

Brent fell back against the hospital bed, reeling from the pain, and the aching in his head, which was swimming in a cocktail of pain killers. The doctor made some notes as the nurse checked Brent's vital signs on the monitor. "You've got four broken ribs, a broken nose, and a lot of bruising, but we are going to take care of everything. Don't worry, you'll be back to normal in no time," said the doctor, as he shot the syringe into Brent's IV tube. Brent looked up at the doctor, and tried to speak, but he slowly faded into sleep.

* * *

Sharp pangs of pain accompanied the blurry face of Jack Ruder as Brent came to.

"George, is he?" Jack shook his head.

"They're saying it's an accident. Passed away in his sleep."

"Of course they are," said Brent, trying to sit up, then he fell back, grimacing."

"Here, use the controls," said Jack, handing him the bed controls. "The cops picked up that religious lunatic for beating you up."

"Banks? It's not him."

"That's not what he says."

"He confessed? Shit, Jack, he's a nut."

"Well, did you see who it was?"

"No, they had masks."

"Well, then…"

"I know it's not him. He's not big enough. Besides, he threatened to shoot me, not beat me up. These guys were big – strong."

Brent coughed, and a searing, burning pain shot to his head from the rib cage through the spine.

"This hurts like hell. So they got my files, identified George as a viable witness, and took him out."

"We don't know that."

"Right. Where's April?"

"At the cop shop now, pleading her case."

"I should go to her." Brent tried to move again, but his body was not cooperating.

"Whoa, wait a minute. You're not going anywhere. I'll go."

"Take Angela with you. She might be able to help somehow."

"I'll ask."

"Everything's gone? My hard drives, the laptop?"

"Yeah. Here," said Jack, holding out a brand new laptop. "I picked up one for you. Knew you'd want to get right back to it."

"Thanks. What about my phone?"

"Found it on you. It's on the table by your bed." Brent looked over and saw the phone.

"Great."

"And I loaded the back-up drive you gave me into the new laptop."

"Well, then all is not lost. I'm only missing a month of work now."

"If anyone can…"

"Right. Bring April over to me as soon as you can."

"I will."

One of the rules of the lawyering game that Brent had learned from his mentor, Charles Stinson, was not to get emotionally attached to a case or a client. But, God damn it, this had gone too far. So far he had lost his best friend, had the shit kicked out of him, his star witness had been killed and his case entirely screwed up. *Fuck the rules,* he thought, *someone has to pay.*

29

On a rare cloudy day for Santa Barbara, before the elegant altar under the golden cupola of the appropriately named *Our Lady of Sorrows Church*, lay the coffin of George Marsh; devoted father, husband, and the latest victim of Prudent Bank. The tearful ceremony was highlighted by the poignant eulogy given by April Marsh, who described a great man whom Brent had never really known, followed by a poem by Mary Elizabeth Frye.

Do not stand at my grave and weep,

I am not there; I do not sleep.

I am a thousand winds that blow,

I am the diamond glints on snow.

I am the sunlight on ripened grain,

I am the gentle autumn rain.

When you awaken in the morning's hush

I am the swift, uplifting rush

Of quiet birds in circled flight.

I am the soft stars that shine at night.

Do not stand at my grave and cry,

I am not there; I did not die.

As Brent and Jack held the rails of George Marsh's casket on the way out of the church, they each made a silent promise to him that justice would be done.

***

The clang of the sally port door slamming brought back unpleasant memories to Brent as the first door closed and he waited for the second door to open to the visiting room at the Santa Barbara County Jail. After Brent had passed the bar exam, Charles Stinson put him on the public defender's list for appointed counsel for parole violators. The memory of the scummy feeling that he felt looking into the empty eyes of thieves, rapists and child molesters came creeping back like a black shadow as Brent walked into the visiting room and took a seat at a window. After about five minutes, a deputy led Joshua Banks, dressed in scrubs, to a small stool on the opposite side of the glass and handcuffed his ankle to it.

"Hello, Mr. Banks."

Banks cocked his little head right, then left, as if he was examining Brent. The grey stubble on his chin matched the fuzz on top of his skull cap, and his stormy grey eyes seemed to focus somewhere in the distance, instead of on Brent's.

"Ah, the heathen has come. What say you, non-believer?"

"Mr. Banks, I know you weren't the one who beat me up."

"I am sworn before God to strike you down, heretic."

"But you didn't strike me down this time, did you, Mr. Banks? Why did you confess to something you didn't do?"

Banks continued to speak in riddled verse. "The Lord works in mysterious ways. God sends His angels to do His bidding."

"So, were you or were you not one of the two men who attacked me in my office?"

"Be gone, demon, I must continue my quest."

"Mr. Banks, this is not a game. People have been killed. You need to tell the truth."

"Of course. The truth shall be revealed to every man."

159

That meeting was about as helpful to Brent as another punch in his already tender ribcage. One thing was for certain, and that was that the police had closed the case and nobody would be looking for the two who really beat him up.

* * *

Brent rose as Angela entered the patio at the El Paseo restaurant, and held her chair as she sat down. She graciously slipped into her chair, keeping her soft, sympathetic eyes trained on Brent.

"There's really no need to be so formal, especially for an injured man," she quipped.

"A lovely lady such as you mandates a sacrifice."

"How are you feeling? I see the black eyes are fading away."

"The ribs are the worst thing. I can't seem to find a comfortable position to sleep in."

The Waiter brought an iron platter of steaming, sizzling fajitas to the table, along with a generous accompaniment of rice, beans and cheese. Angela prepared one for each of them as Brent nursed his Margarita.

"Brent, I think this case is becoming much too dangerous."

"It was dangerous from the start."

"But I worry for you if it continues this way."

"I can't quit, Angela, not now. Too much has been lost."

"I know."

"I think we should try to match those hair fibers you found to the two men who followed me," said Brent.

"Is this another hunch?"

"I guess you could call it that."

"The problem is that we have no probable cause to search them."

"What if they were to get arrested for something?"

"Brent, what's bubbling in your brain besides that frozen Margarita?"

"Just asking."

"Of course, depending on the crime they were accused of, we could take samples while they were in custody. I could arrange that."

***

Visiting scumbags in jail was not the only remnant of Brent's former life as a poor man's lawyer. He had also done more than a few divorces for bikers and their biker bitches. Of the many offers Brent had received during those

161

times, many included lines of coke or lids of weed in return for legal services, which he politely declined. But the most interesting offer was a "biker party." Basically, for a case or a keg of beer, an entire biker gang would show up at the home of your "friend" and have a party, driving motorcycles in and out of the house, swimming naked in your swimming pool, trashing your living room, and spinning donuts on your front lawn with their hogs. Of course, Brent had always declined these offers as well, but there was a particular job he thought suitable for these ex-clients, who owed him numerous favors.

Brent waited in his car at Tucker's Grove Park. The unmistakable distinctive sound of a Harley Davidson preceded the dust cloud as the bearded, pot-bellied biker road up to Brent's window. Letting the hog idle, the biker smiled a mouthful of yellow teeth.

"Hey counselor. You've looked better."

"Thanks. Now, remember, nothing criminal. You just verbally provoke them and let them start the fight."

"Nothing criminal? What fun would that be? And no repeat business for you, counselor."

"You promised."

"Yeah, yeah, you got the envelope?"

Brent handed the guy a manila envelope containing pictures of the two suspects and all the information that Jack was able to obtain on them. He snatched it, revved his hog, and gave a salute to Brent as he rode off.

30

Like the sand slips through the hourglass, time slips through your fingers. The trial was less than five weeks away, and those weeks had a peculiar way of turning into days, then hours, then minutes. By the same token, Brent's long hours at the office turned the days into nights and the nights into days. It was dark when he arrived to the office in the morning, and it was dark when he left it at night. So, the call from Angela at 7 p.m. was just what he needed.

"Hey Brent, you're working too hard," she said. "Why don't you take a break and meet me for dinner?"

"Are you asking me out?"

"Why don't you meet me and find out?"

"Now that sounds intriguing. Where?"

"How about my place? I think a bachelor like you could use a home cooked meal. Around 8?"

Brent had barely enough time to shower, shave and dress for dinner. With his regular caseload and the trial preparations, and the loss of Rick, his lunches with Angela had evolved into being his only social life. He often found that his thoughts drifted in her direction before he closed his eyes to sleep every night.

* * *

Angela's apartment was a two-level in a Spanish style building with a beautiful stone paved courtyard that contained a garden exploding with flowers of all colors and a fountain in the center. Brent parked his car out front, and took a bottle of wine and red roses from the passenger's seat that he had bought on the way. As he passed through the courtyard, the scent of the roses was overpowered by jasmine and plumeria. Brent found Angela's apartment and knocked on the door.

"Flowers!" she exclaimed when she opened the door. "And wine! You are truly a gentleman, Mr. Marks."

"Thank you," Brent said as Angela showed him in.

"Now, sit down and relax. No working tonight."

"Okay doctor."

"And give me your cell phone."

Brent reluctantly complied. But, just as Angela went to switch it off, he said, "What if someone calls?"

"Brent, there's a new technology. Perhaps you've heard of it. It's called voice mail."

Brent chuckled and figured, *what the hell.*

31

To the novice, it may have appeared that a storm was rolling down Stagecoach Road, accompanied by dark clouds and the roar of thunder. But it was not an act of God; rather a pack of hogs rolling into the Cold Spring Tavern Saturday night. The clan of bearded men and tattooed women rumbled in on their bikes, peeled their leather coated bodies off their saddles, and packed into the bar area.

Fifteen minutes later, the beer flowed and sweaty, bearded riders told riding stories, while their biker bitches gathered in sewing circles around the tables. The door opened and a lone, clean shaven white man in jeans with no leather pushed through the crowd and had a seat at the bar. He was physically fit, confident, and tall. Looking around, he realized that he fit in about as well as a watermelon in a pumpkin field.

"What brings you here, friend?" said the pot-bellied biker on his left. The man ignored the faux-friendly advance, and ordered a beer.

"Dude, I'm talkin' to you. Ain't you got no manners?" The biker got in his face.

"Get lost, dirt bag, I didn't come here to socialize."

"Then why did you come here, you little faggot? Can't you see they only allow real men in here?"

The stranger regarded him with snake-eyes, cold and calculated. "Look, you fat fuck. You think I'm afraid of you and your dickless little biker buddies? Back off. I won't say it again."

As another equally out of place meatneck entered the tavern, he recognized the stranger at the bar and sat down next to him.

"Why the fuck did you pick this biker hangout to meet me?" asked the meatneck.

"What are you talking about? You left a message to meet me here," said the stranger.

About the time they realized they had been had, a small circle of beards had come to surround them at the bar area. The stranger threw a fiver on the bar and stood up, as did his meatneck friend.

"You boys leavin' without apologizing to my friend?" asked a bearded leather mountain.

The stranger had no fear. "Tell your buddies to move their gang bang over and let us pass," he commanded. The mountain man just moved closer.

"Didn't you hear my friend, Harley? Step aside, we're leaving," said the meatneck.

"It's a good thing, Nancy," said the mountain. We don't take kindly to no fudge pushers meetin' their faggy friends in our bar."

Meatneck snapped, and grabbed the mountain's hand, twisted it, and slammed it down on the bar. "Maybe I didn't make myself clear," he spit, through clenched teeth.

The mountain man just flashed a big grin of tobacco stained teeth, as if he felt no pain at all. "You drew first blood," he said, as he grabbed the meatneck by the back of the head and slammed it against the bar.

The meatneck sprang up from the bar with incredible strength, ripping through the mountain man's vice-like grip and struck at him and three other men like a caged-in cobra. His partner, the stranger, became a whirling dervish, kicking, punching and spitting, and knocking out one biker after another, until he reached the mountain man, who had already been kicked down by his partner.

In a devilish frenzy, the two took turns kicking the fat man into a pulp while his biker friends tried to come to his aid. They threw off the first three bikers, then spun around, back to back and flashed knives to the circle. "This party's over," said the meatneck. "Now back the fuck off unless you want to join your fat friend on his fucking back."

The bikers did as instructed. As the two misfits made their way to the door, the riders came to the aid of the moaning mountain man.

Suddenly, four cops in riot gear entered the bar. "Nobody move!" said the lead cop. Upon quickly ascertaining who the victims were and who were the perpetrators, two cops handcuffed the two intruders, and pushed them out the door, while the other two cops took statements from the bikers. Two EMT's ran in with a gurney and started working on the mountain man. Clearly visible in his fist was a clump of hair.

32

There comes a point in time when deadlines catch up to preparations and you realize that you can never be prepared enough. Compare a trial to a battle of gladiators in the ancient Roman Colosseum, in which two gladiators (the lawyers) fight to the death, to entertain the spectators. In this game, a prepared mind is more important than anything else.

Brent's case was about as strong as a paper bag. His star witness was dead, and the only choice he had to present that testimony was to show the video tape of the deposition or read the dry transcript into the record. It would take a great deal of theatrics to get the jury to return a RICO verdict against the bank. But the first obstacle would be Joe Stein's motion in limine to exclude the deposition transcript and the video tape from even being presented.

Judge Virginia Masters took the bench at exactly 8:30 a.m. Every minute of each of the six days of the trial had been allocated, and each side's time for presenting evidence as well as the time for argument, had been divvied out and accounted for up to the last second. Brent felt sorry for her husband.

"This is the trial of Marsh v. Prudent Bank, case Number CV 13 – 61940. Counsel please state your appearances."

"Good morning, Your Honor. Brent Marks appearing for the Plaintiff."

"Good morning, Mr. Marks."

"Good morning, Your Honor. Joe Stein appearing for Defendant Prudent Bank."

"Good morning, Mr. Stein."

"Good morning, Your Honor. William Black appearing for Defendant Steven Bernstein."

"Good morning, Mr. Black. There are two motions pending before this Court. First is Defendants' motion to dismiss the Plaintiff's case due to the death of George Marsh, the principal Plaintiff. My tentative ruling is to deny the motion. Clearly the causes of action touching and concerning the property flow with the property. Therefore, his daughter, his only heir and the executrix of his estate, can maintain them.

With regard to the RICO claim, it is a little more complicated. Although there is no Ninth Circuit law on the subject, Mr. Marks points out that at least one Circuit Court of Appeal, in the case of *Faircloth v. Finesod,* has ruled that RICO is a remedial statute and that Congress intended it to survive the death of the Plaintiff. I tend to concur with this decision. The floor is now yours, Mr. Stein."

After a limited 15 minutes of argument on the part of Joe Stein, and rebuttal by Brent, the judge's tentative ruling stood, and Brent looked confidently at April, who was sitting next to him at the counsel table, silently basking in the victory. But it was a victory short lived.

"Regarding the Defendants' joint motion to exclude the deposition of George Marsh," said Judge Masters, "I have read the motion and supporting documentation and the opposition. My tentative ruling is to grant the motion. There is no case law which authorizes the presentation of evidence by argumentative or alternative communication, and it would be confusing enough to the jury to have Mr. Marsh present his testimony live, let alone posthumously by video tape."

Brent's heart dropped through his stomach. He had lost the first battle before having the opportunity to fire one shot.

"Mr. Marks, I will hear from you," said Her Majesty.

"Yes. Thank you, Your Honor. As the Court will note from the authority I have filed with my opposition, augmentative and alternative communication as interpreted by Mr. Marsh's doctor is no different than allowing an interpreter to present testimony by a person who does not speak English."

"Come on, Mr. Marks, you can't expect Mr. Stein and Mr. Black to be able to cross-examine a witness effectively under these circumstances."

"On the contrary, Your Honor, they already have. I hardly got the chance to ask Mr. Marsh a question during the deposition. Most of the questioning consisted of their cross-examination."

"But it is not a different language; it's Mr. Marsh's own special language that he and his doctor have invented."

"Actually, Your Honor, as you can see from the declaration of Dr. Senlon, the basis of their communication is very simple, and utilizes a communication board with an English alphabet.

In my brief, I cited the case of *Vasquez v. Kirkland,* a Ninth Circuit case, where the witness in that case was deaf, and communicated with a set of gestures and facial expressions, which were interpreted by another deaf person in sign language to a court certified interpreter who then translated the sign language to the jury. The Court held that the jury, having been instructed about the process, could put the weight on the testimony that it saw fit. In light of that decision and the others cited in my brief, it would be improper to exclude his testimony, especially now that he has passed away."

"Mr. Stein?"

"Thank you, Your Honor. The defense agrees with the Court's tentative ruling. This case is a far cry from *Vasquez*. In Vasquez, a certified court translator did the interpreting, not the witness's psychologist."

"Mr. Marks?"

"Your Honor, I agree that this is not exactly the same case as *Vasquez*. In Vasquez, the witness's testimony went through two filters of interpretation. In Mr. Marsh's deposition, there was only one. That makes it even more reliable than the testimony in the *Vasquez* case. Moreover, at Mr. Marsh's deposition, Dr. Senlon, who is an expert in augmentative and alternative communication, testified under oath about the process as it applied to Mr. Marsh, and her interpretation of the communication can be relied upon as expert testimony."

"Your Honor, if I may," said Stein. "Counsel is trying to shove an entirely new method of communication down the Court's throat. It is not another language. It is not sign language, and Mr. Marsh was not deaf."

"Your Honor, 47 states including our own, and the District of Columbia allow public funding of augmentative and alternative communication devices. In *William T. ex rel. Gigi T. v. Taylor,* the District Court held that Medicare programs should cover these devices. This is nothing new," argued Brent.

"Plus his doctor, who is an expert in this method of communication and who designed the system of communication will testify as an expert witness. The United States Supreme Court in *Daubert v. Merrell Dow Pharmaceuticals* in 1993 established requirements for admissibility of expert testimony, including whether or not the employed technique has been peer-reviewed and published, has a known error rate, can be tested, and is a generally accepted practice within the field. Dr. Senlon will testify that augmentative and alternative communication of this kind is a generally accepted practice in her field."

"Gentlemen, I have read your briefs, now I would like to watch a portion of the video tape so that I can make a determination. Court is adjourned for two hours."

* * *

"What does it mean?" April interrogated Brent at the counsel table.

"It means we have a 50-50 chance of getting her to change her mind, but she's going to decide it on her own, after she watches the tape."

"And if she excludes it?"

178

"No RICO, no mortgage fraud. We need his testimony to establish the elements of our case."

"I should have never attacked them. Dad's dead, your friend is missing, and it's all for nothing."

April sobbed, gasped for air, and the streams turned into rivers. Brent put his arm around her to comfort her.

"Don't cry. Let's wait and see what happens. If she denies it, we go through the trial and appeal. If she doesn't, we're back in the game."

Thus began the longest two hours in the history of Marsh v Prudent Bank.

33

When the buzzer rang in the courtroom, signaling the entrance of Judge Masters, it was as silent as a church. All eyes were on the judge as she took the bench.

"Back on the record in Marsh versus Prudent Bank. I have read and considered all papers in support of Defendant's motion in limine, and the opposition, considered the argument of counsel, and watched two hours of the videotaped deposition. I have decided to reverse my tentative ruling and to deny the motion. The jury can decide what weight, if any to give the testimony."

Stein sprang up from his seat. "Your Honor, may I be heard, please?"

"No, Mr. Stein, you may not. I have made my decision. Are there any further matters for the Court to consider before proceeding to jury selection?"

"No."

"No."

"Very well then, the clerk will send in the jury panel."

* * *

Brent was looking for jurors whose lives had been touched by foreclosure or loan fraud. It was a good bet that Stein would not allow any juror to remain on the panel who had any direct experience with foreclosure; but Brent was looking for subtleties – people who had fallen on hard times and felt the demon of foreclosure breathing at their neck, but somehow had made it. Or people whose family member had been touched by foreclosure. These potential jurors would have a hard time feeling sorry for Prudent Bank in this case. Brent gave the panel list to Jack, who did a quick background check to determine who may potentially fall into these categories.

Potential jurors from the panel were called up 12 at a time, and sat in the jury box to endure the process of "voir dire," a kind of cross-examination of their backgrounds. Stein's questioning nitpicked at the financial background of each potential juror, looking for proud hard working men and women who had always been able to pay their bills and would not tend to see someone who had not paid their mortgage as a victim.

Finally, Brent used up the last of his allotted voir dire time, with two possible wild card jurors still left in the jury box – Franklin Thomas, a middle-aged black factory worker who probably would never be able to afford his own home, and Claire Deans, a single mother.

Neither one of them had suffered a foreclosure at the hands of a predatory lender, but the background checks revealed that Thomas had paid his share of high interest loans on rent to own furniture and car payments. Deans had grown up in Lancaster, California, a small bedroom community north of Los Angeles, which was one of the hardest hit communities by the foreclosure crisis. She was likely to have at least one friend who had suffered a foreclosure. Satisfied with the jury, Brent announced, "The Plaintiff will accept the jury as presently constituted."

That left about twenty minutes to Stein before the lunch break. However, to Brent's surprise, Stein also announced that he would accept the jury. The Clerk swore in the jury, and the judge gave them the beginning admonishments not to discuss the case outside of the jury room or with any counsel.

"Your Honor, may counsel approach the bench?" asked Stein.

The request was granted and, outside the presence of the jury, Stein asked, "Your Honor, may we have a small recess before lunch? I have an important matter to discuss with my client that may be dispositive of the case."

"Well, Mr. Stein, we have about fifteen minutes left before the lunch break, and, as you know, I have all the time for this trial carefully allotted out. There won't be any more time in the schedule to give."

"I know, Your Honor, but it is critical that I contact my client immediately, before the lunch break."

"I'm not inclined to grant that, but if you want to break for lunch early, that fifteen minutes will count against your allotted time, and I'm sure Mr. Marks will be happy to discuss any issues you feel may be dispositive of this case."

"I'll wait in the hall," said Brent."

34

One of the tenets of trial preparation was to be ready for just about anything to happen. Although the rules of discovery left no surprises in the evidence, that didn't mean that there were no surprises at all during trial. Sometimes witnesses didn't testify in the same way or with the same demeanor. Trial was an art, not a science, and the outcomes were less predictable than any science experiment could ever be. Brent was curious about what Stein had to say that may have the magnitude to dispose of the entire case, but not surprised. The rulings on the motion in limine had come as a great blow to him. Brent's case was weak at best, and depended on putting on the video tape of George Marsh's testimony, but it was still a case that could be presented to the jury, who would decide it not by logic, but with emotion. Stein and his client had obviously made an economic assessment and decided it how much it was worth to them to end it all now with a settlement offer. Stein approached Brent, who was sitting on a bench outside the courtroom. He sat next to him and offered one of his phony smiles.

"Brent, I have an offer from my client, but it's the only one we're prepared to make, so I suggest you discuss it with your client thoroughly."

"What's the offer?"

"Any settlement would have to be confidential."

This meant that neither April nor Brent could ever discuss the settlement, or the case. It could also not be a "calling card" for Brent's specializing in predatory lending cases.

"I'm listening," said Brent.

"We will stipulate to quiet title to the house and discharge the loan. Your client walks away with her parents' house and we eat the mortgage. Both sides to pay their own fees and costs."

"Not sure if that will fly, but I'll communicate it to my client."

"Let me know before she takes the bench and we'll put it on the record."

***

Brent called April and told her to meet him at the Carl's Junior in the Los Angeles Mall, and made his way across the street, taking the first available orange plastic booth, which was covered with a layer of wiped-over grease. A few seconds later, a man sat down at his table. He was about 50, with short, greying hair, slate grey eyes and an ample nose. He was dressed about the same as the other patrons; like a government worker who was taking a lunch break from work.

"I'm afraid this seat is taken," said Brent.

"Don't worry, Mr. Marks, I won't be long," said the stranger, in a scratchy, but distinguished voice that bore an East Coast accent.

"I'm sorry, but I don't know you. Who are you?"

"I represent an interested party in the Marsh case."

"And that party would be?"

"That's confidential."

"And your name?"

"You can call me Mike."

"Okay, Mike. I don't know who you are or who this interested party is, but I'm meeting my client in a few minutes, and I'd like to ask you to leave."

"Look, Mr. Marks. We all have our jobs to do..."

"And yours is?"

"I take care of the things that need to get done. And I'm very good at what I do."

That sounded like a threat to Brent, but this guy looked more like a businessman than a thug.

"Great, now, as I said, I'm meeting my client, and..."

"Mr. Marks, I know you don't know me and think you have no reason to talk to me, but let me assure you of one thing. Talking to me right now is the most important thing you may do in your life."

Brent looked at the stranger with surprise, but he continued without letting Brent get a word in. "My employer has an interest in this case settling. Whether it settles now or later is not important, but it must be settled. Am I making myself clear?" The stranger's resolve and the look in his eyes as they made burning contact with Brent's felt both mysterious and dangerous.

"I'm not sure I understand."

"If this case were not to settle, that would be a mess...a mess that I would be charged with cleaning up. You are familiar with the function of a cleaner, Mr. Marks, aren't you?" The mystery that Brent was feeling suddenly turned to terror, and crawled its way up his spine.

"I think I get the message," said Brent.

"I thought you would. Have a nice day, Mr. Marks." The stranger rose.

"Wait, how do I contact you?"

"Mr. Marks, if you do the right thing, this should be the last time you ever need to have contact with me." And with that, the stranger left. Brent turned his head to look, but the stranger, Mike, had disappeared.

John Kennedy said, "In a crisis, be aware of the danger, but recognize the opportunity." Brent had been handed an opportunity to settle the case and now it was clear to him just how dangerous this case really was.

35

"You honestly think I'm going to accept this?" April demanded. Her attitude seethed and catapulted toward Brent as if he was not only the bearer, but the producer of the bad news.

"April, have you heard of the cliché 'Don't shoot the messenger?' Firstly, I have a legal obligation to convey this offer to you. Secondly, no more than five minutes after Stein gave me the offer, I was visited by a 'friend of an interested party' who encouraged me to accept it."

"What do you mean?"

"Would it surprise you, April, after your father's death and the certain murder of my investigator, that a criminal element may be at play here?"

"It's Bernstein, I know it is."

"No matter who it is, the fact is that we are both in danger. You and me. And there's nothing that anyone can do to protect us. We have to take that into account in evaluating this offer."

"I don't accept it."

"Remember what I told you in the beginning? That if we invalidate their right to foreclose, you still owe them money if you want to keep the house? Accepting this offer means you don't owe the money anymore. You were the one who told me, just today, that you should have never taken on the bank."

"Yes, but…"

"Let's think about this logically. We might be able to swing it if we brought a videotaped deposition of a deceased witness who could speak, but your father's testimony is shaky at best even if he were still alive to give it, because of the issue of augmentative and alternative communication."

"But we won on that issue…"

"Yes, because I convinced the judge to go against her tentative ruling. But if she had a problem with it initially, just imagine what the 12 strangers on the jury will think about it."

"So you think I should take the offer? Even with them cramming it down our throats like this? And threatening us as well?"

"You decide. I'm just delivering the facts. They may be bluffing, but chances are that they're not. Winning a case is not worth your life."

"This case is."

"This case has already cost you, April, and RICO is our shakiest cause of action. We have a 50-50 chance at best to win it."

"Then why would they offer a settlement?"

"We have a better than 50-50 chance on our declaratory relief action. They know that. It won't cost them anything to walk away from the loan. And they're afraid of that 50% chance we could get RICO. It would be a disaster for them."

"I need time to think about it."

"That's one thing we don't have."

"Then let's keep going."

* * *

Standing at the lectern in front of the jury box, Brent's opening statement was short and to the point, as he outlined the evidence that he intended to present in his case-in-chief. However, to spoon feed twelve people who were either forced to jury duty, or appearing there instead of being on their job, he had to hook them within the first five minutes, which were carefully calculated to make the trial interesting. As he spoke, he made eye contact with every juror.

"Ladies and Gentlemen, in 2008, the United States economy and the world economy crashed as a direct result of widespread bank fraud, taking many victims with it, including my client's parents, George and Anne Marsh, who were brutally beaten in their home on November 25, 2008.

"April's mother, Anne, was murdered. Her father, George Marsh, was incapacitated from injuries received in the beating and he has recently died. We will present evidence in this trial that Prudent Bank was responsible for their personal tragedy."

Brent paused to look at April, then back at the jury.

"To understand what happened, you have to first understand how the banks in general, and Tentane Mutual in particular contributed to the financial crisis of 2008, in which many people had lost almost everything they owned, including their homes, large financial institutions almost collapsed, and stock markets throughout the world crashed.

"The big banks made loans on real estate that was overvalued. Those loans were designed to start at very low interest rates, and the rates could then fluctuate and go exponentially higher. In this way, many people were qualified for loans but they could not afford to pay in the long run. Finally, those loans were pooled together and packaged as securities called mortgage backed securities that were sold by Wall Street to investors. This way, the banks made huge fees, brokers made enormous commissions, and the risk was passed on to investors in the market."

Brent paused, looked down at his notes, then back at Juror number 6, Claire Deans, to begin his eyeball journey back and forth across the jury box, ending with juror 12, Franklin Thomas. The subject was a bit dry, but the jury was hooked.

"The financial crisis was triggered by a complex interplay of relaxed lending policies by the big banks that made getting a home loan easier, and overvalued sub-prime mortgages which were pooled and sold to investors as mortgage backed securities. They overvalued properties based of their mistaken theory that housing prices would always continue to escalate. If you had a house, you could get a loan. It was that simple.

"Add to this questionable trading practices on behalf of both buyers and sellers, compensation structures that prioritized short-term deal flow over long-term value, and a lack of adequate capital holdings from banks and insurance companies to secure or back the financial commitments they were making, and you had a disaster that was just waiting to happen. For George and Anne Marsh their own personal disaster began when they were offered a loan by Tentane Mutual, through Steven Bernstein, its Santa Barbara loan manager."

Brent went on to outline the evidence that he would present in the case, which pointed to the conclusion that Tentane Mutual had failed to assign the Marsh loan to the trust securitization pool before it closed, thus rendering the assignment to the trust invalid under the agreement that had set it up. Prudent Bank tried to cover up this failure by fraudulently assigning it to the trust securitization pool after they found out it had never been done. This meant that Prudent had no right to foreclose on the property. Brent then went on to the grand prize – RICO.

"We intend to present evidence that Prudent Bank has committed at least two serious crimes; the crime of financial institution fraud and the crime of aiding and abetting murder."

The wide-opened eyes and mouths of most of the men and women of the jury indicated to Brent that, if they were asleep before, they had now awakened. Nobody could resist a good murder mystery. They kept their eyes on Brent as if they were watching a compelling docudrama on television, as he outlined the evidence he would present in the case, despite the intermittent objections by Stein to try to throw Brent off.

William Black took the podium next to present his statement of the case for Steven Bernstein. His skill and manner of presentation gave away his undeniable experience as a trial attorney, shattering any hopes Brent may have had for the jury to get bored by the time Stein took to give his opening remarks.

36

Shakespeare must have had a courtroom in mind when he said, "All the world's a stage," and Joe Stein confidently took that stage like it was his kingdom. His manner in speaking to the jury made everyone in the room feel like they were sitting in front of the fireplace at Stein's house, while he told a tantalizing story.

"Good morning ladies and gentlemen. It is certainly a tragedy that April Marsh lost both of her parents, in such a terrible way and at such a young age."

Stein feigned a genuine look of sympathy in April's direction.

"I'm not going to play down the evidence of her tragic loss. But that is not what this case is about. The evidence I will present here will show that Tentane Mutual and then Prudent

Bank offered their help to George Marsh when he was in despair and at his greatest time of need."

Brent could have sworn he heard an orchestra of violins playing a melancholy tune while Stein cleverly used the Marsh tragedy to set up the bank, not as the evil Simon Legree, but the hero who had come to their rescue.

"Ladies and Gentlemen, the evidence will show that all of the documents were properly recorded that were necessary to secure the Marsh note, and that this note was passed on to Prudent Bank. I agree with Mr. Marks that it is a terrible thing to lose your home, but the evidence in this case will show that Mr. and Mrs. Marsh voluntarily put their home up as collateral for the money they so desperately needed to get their financial lives back on track. They knew the risk if the unspeakable happened; if things didn't work out and they were unable to pay the loan."

Stein cleverly weaved in every fact he intended to produce, and the jury, rather than being bored, was absolutely fixated on his version of the story.

"Ladies and Gentlemen, finally I would like to remind you that it is the Plaintiff who must bear the burden of bringing forth evidence to support each of her claims. Think of it as a puzzle. We all know what a puzzle looks like if it's only missing a few pieces here and there. We can still tell what the picture is. But if the puzzle is missing too many pieces, it's impossible to recognize the picture without looking at the box. What does not fit in this puzzle is the act of murder. And, like that unfinished and undiscernible puzzle, even though I believe that the evidence the Plaintiff produces will not be enough to make a case of RICO, we will present evidence that negates the bank of any responsibility."

When Stein had finished, Brent realized that Stein had planted seeds in the minds of each of the jurors that he would cultivate and water during the trial. The jurors had now been briefed. All of their biases and prejudices, their first impressions of April, Brent, Stein, and Black and Bernstein, had all been fixed in stone. Whether the evidence that was presented could change any of those pre-formulated opinions would not be known until the end of the trial.

37

"Mr. Marks, you may call your first witness, said Judge Masters.

"The Plaintiff calls Tanya Barton."

Barton was a custodian of records for Prudent Bank. She was short, timid, and was dressed in a 90's style business suit, as if she had recently purchased her wardrobe at the Goodwill or had just forgotten to take it there. Her testimony, although dry, was essential to establishing the elements of the case.

Barton testified that in 2006, Tentane Mutual had loaned $750,000 to the Marshes, and identified their loan application, the subprime promissory note and deed of trust. She also verified that the note contained an adjustable rate rider allowing the interest rate to adjust, or increase, on the first day of June 2006 and on that day every month thereafter for the entire life of the loan. With Barton's testimony, Brent had established that the Marshes had taken out a subprime, toxic loan with Tentane that had provisions for "death spiral" interest rate increases that would make it impossible for them to pay their payments later on. Later, Brent would call Bernstein to testify that he prequalified the Marshes for this loan, even though they had no income at the time.

Barton further identified the Pooling and Service Agreement (PSA) that Tentane had entered into with Deutschland Bank, which was governed by New York law, and the trust it created that was called "Tentane Mutual Pass-Through Certificates, Mortgage Series 2006-TT53 Trust." The intention of Tentane was to transfer the Marsh loan into the trust along with hundreds of millions of dollars in other mortgages, take the money, and then forget about them.

Altogether, the trust would hold over $2 billion in mortgages, which would be sold off to investors as mortgage backed securities in a virtual free for all. Barton read into the record that portion of the Pooling and Service Agreement that required any transfer of any mortgage or deed of trust to be before the closing date of the trust.

"Ms. Barton, can you please tell the Court when the closing date of the trust was?"

"August 20, 2006."

"And when was the Marsh loan transferred to the trust?"

"It was transferred by assignment on September 26, 2008."

"Objection and move to strike," barked Stein. "Ms. Marsh has no standing to raise any issue with regard to the assignment."

"Counsel, please approach the bench with the Court reporter," said Judge Masters. All the lawyers and the reporter came to the bench, outside the earshot of the jury.

"Your Honor," said Stein. "The Marshes were not privy to the Pooling Service Agreement, and it is not relevant to the issues of this case. Ms. Marsh has no standing to enforce the terms of the Agreement. "

"Mr. Marks, how does your client have standing to raise the issue of the assignment to the trust?"

"Your Honor, if the assignment was made after the closing date of the trust, then Prudent Bank lacks the legal right to enforce the note. I cite *Glaski v. Bank of America*, 218 Cal. App. 4th 1079."

"Your Honor," said Stein, "Neither the Plaintiff nor her parents were primary parties nor were they third party beneficiaries with respect to the pooling service agreement, and have no standing to enforce the terms of the PSA."

"What about that Mr. Marks?"

"Your Honor, this is a declaratory relief action. If the transfer to the PSA was void because it was made after the closing, then nobody seeking to enforce that deed of trust who claims ownership or servicing rights pursuant to the PSA has the right to foreclose."

"Good point, Mr. Marks. Consistent with the *Glaski* case, I will allow it in, and leave it for the jury to decide its weight."

All counsel took their places in the courtroom.

"You may proceed, Mr. Marks."

"The assignment occurred over two years after the closing date of the trust, correct?"

"It appears so, yes."

"Calling your attention to Exhibit 5, can you identify this document?"

"Yes, that is the assignment of the Marsh deed of trust to the Tentane Mutual Pass-Through Certificates, Mortgage Series 2006-TT53 Trust."

"Thank you. Your Honor. I move that Exhibit 5 be admitted into evidence."

"Exhibit 5 is received."

Brent next had Barton identify the Notice of Default on the Marshes' deed of trust, which began a 90 day default period, and the Notice of

Trustee's Sale, which began a 21 day period, the last day of which would be the foreclosure sale.

"Your Honor, I move Exhibits 6 and 7 into evidence."

"Any objection? Exhibits 6 and 7 are admitted."

Brent had already established that the Marshes' loan had been transferred to the trust by Tentane Mutual after the closing of the trust. He went on to have Barton identify all of the filings of the trust with the S.E.C., which showed that Tentane Mutual had sold all of the deeds of trust in the trust to various investors as mortgage backed securities.

"Now, Ms. Barton, I am showing you what has been marked collectively as Exhibit 9. Can you identify these documents?"

"It looks like the payment and collection records on the Marsh loan from Tentane Mutual."

"And Exhibit 10?"

"Exhibit 10 appears to be the payment and collection records on the Marsh loan from Prudent Bank."

"And from these records, can you determine who now services and collects payments under the Marsh loan?"

"Prudent Bank services the loan and collects any payments made on it."

"Thank you Ms. Barton. Your Honor, I move Exhibits 9 and 10 into evidence."

"No objection? They are received."

"Finally, Ms. Barton, can you please identify Exhibit 11?"

Barton flipped through Exhibit 11, which was voluminous.

"Exhibit 11 appears to be the Agreement with the FDIC for the purchase of the assets of Tentane Mutual by Prudent Bank."

"And is this your certification on Exhibit 12 that Exhibit 11 is a true copy of that agreement?"

"It is."

"Your Honor, I move that Exhibits 11 and 12 be admitted into evidence."

"Any objection, Mr. Stein? 11 and 12 are admitted."

"Ms. Barton, can you please identify Exhibit 13?"

"Yes. Exhibit 13 is a letter from Adelay Gioriano, the collection manager of Prudent Bank."

"And what do your records show was the purpose of this letter?"

"To tell Mr. and Mrs. Marsh that Prudent had taken over their loan and to send further payments to Prudent Bank."

Brent moved the exhibit into evidence and it was admitted.

"Thank you, Ms. Barton. No further questions, Your Honor," said Brent.

Brent knew that Stein would not benefit from asking any questions on cross-examination about most of the paperwork that was in evidence, and he couldn't risk boring the jury any further, or emphasizing anything that was potentially damaging. However, since the judge had allowed the pooling and service agreement and the late assignment of the Marsh loan into evidence, he had to exercise some damage control.

"Mr. Stein, your witness."

"Thank you, Your Honor. Ms. Barton, I call your attention to Exhibit 3, the pooling and service agreement. That agreement was made in August 2006, is that correct?"

"Objection," said Brent. "The Exhibit speaks for itself."

"It does," said the judge, but this is cross examination. I will allow it."

"Yes, the agreement was made in August 2006," said Barton.

"And the Marsh loan closed in April 2006, isn't that correct?"

"Yes, it did."

"And neither Mr. Marsh nor Mrs. Marsh were parties to the pooling servicing agreement, isn't that correct?"

"Yes."

"So then, since their escrow had already closed, Mr. and Mrs. Marsh were not contemplated by the parties to the pooling service agreement to have any benefits flowing from that agreement, isn't that correct?"

"Objection! Lack of foundation, argumentative and calls for a legal conclusion," said Brent.

"Yes," Barton blurted out.

"Move to strike the answer," said Brent.

"Sustained. The jury will disregard the question and the answer. Ms. Barton, remember what I told you. Wait for the objection to be ruled on before you answer."

Too late, they already heard it. That was Stein's plan. He had taken advantage of the fact that Barton would follow her pattern and jump to the answer before a ruling on the objection.

Confucius said, *Study the past if you would define the future.* Brent should have been prepared to jump in with his objection before the ink had dried on Stein's question. But Barton knew which side she was on. She knew she had to downplay what would be damaging to her employer. Thus, the seed for the defense was planted in each of the 12 brains in the jury box. Brent's job would be to make sure that seed would never grow.

38

"The Plaintiff calls Ms. Adelay Gioriano."

Adelay Gioriano was a low level executive at Prudent Bank, charged with mortgage loan collections. She reluctantly took the witness stand in a floral print skirt with white blouse, and nervously avoided looking at the jury. Brent questioned her on her position with the bank and went over all the documents, then zeroed in for the kill.

"Ms. Gioriano, in September 2008, when Prudent Bank took over the assets of Tentane Mutual, your department performed an inventory of all the mortgage loans that Prudent was taking over, isn't that correct?"

"Yes we did."

"And as part of that inventory, your department performed due diligence on the papers and records of every mortgage loan, isn't that correct?"

"Yes. It was a very big job."

"I'm certain that it was. Now, Ms. Gioriano, you are familiar with Exhibit 3, The Pooling Service Agreement for the Tentane Mutual Pass-Through Certificates, Mortgage Series 2006-TT53 Trust, are you not?"

"I am."

"And, calling your attention to Exhibit 2, this is the assignment of the Marsh mortgage loan to this trust, isn't it?"

"Yes, it appears to be."

"What is the date of the assignment?"

"September 26, 2008."

"And that was by Tentane Mutual to the trust, correct?"

"Yes."

"What was the date of the agreement with the FDIC to take over Tentane's assets?"

"September 25, 2008."

"So Tentane Mutual assigned the Marsh loan to the trust the day after Prudent Bank took over Tentane's assets?"

"Objection argumentative," said Stein.

"Overruled," said Judge Masters.

"I'm not sure," said Gioriano.

"How could you not be sure, Ms. Gioriano? September 26th comes after September 25th usually, doesn't it?"

"Objection, argumentative!" barked Stein.

"Sustained!"

"Now I would like to call your attention to Exhibit 13."

"Okay."

"Is this a letter from you to Mr. and Mrs. Marsh?"

"Yes it is."

"And the date of that letter?"

"September 25, 2008."

"Ms. Gioriano, can you please read the letter into the record?"

"Yes. *Dear Mr. and Mrs. Marsh, I am writing to advise you that, as of September 25, 2008, Prudent Bank has taken over the assets of Tentane Mutual Bank, which assets include the servicing of the above-referenced loan and deed of trust. Please make all future loan payments to the address on the bottom of this letter, and reference your new loan number, which is indicated in the reference section. Welcome to the Prudent Bank family. We look forward to a long and mutually beneficial banking relationship.*"

"Ms. Gioriano, you state in the letter that, as of September 25, 2008, Prudent Bank has taken over the servicing of the Marsh loan and deed of trust, correct?"

"Yes."

"But that's not true, is it?"

"What?"

"It's a false statement, Ms. Gioriano, isn't it?"

"Objection, argumentative," barked Stein.

"Overruled. The witness may answer."

"We did take over Tentane Mutual."

"Yes, but not the Marsh loan, isn't that true?"

"Well, I…"

"Objection!"

"Sustained. Mr. Marks, please rephrase your question."

"The Pooling Service Agreement Trust closed in 2006."

"Yes."

"And the terms of the Pooling Service Agreement that we went over earlier state that all loans must be assigned by the closing of the Trust, correct?"

"Yes."

"This loan was not assigned by the closing date, isn't that correct?"

"It was in our inventory."

"Move to strike as non-responsive."

"Granted," said Masters. "The jury will disregard the answer."

"The loan was not assigned pursuant to the terms of the Pooling Service Agreement, isn't that true?"

"Yes, but…"

"And the assignment states that it was made by Tentane Mutual one day after Prudent took over its assets."

"Yes."

"So, on September 25, 2008 the day your letter went to Mr. and Mrs. Marsh, Prudent Bank did not yet have the right to service their loan, correct?"

"Well, I suppose so. But…"

"And, in fact, Prudent never had the right to service the loan, isn't that true?"

"No that is not true."

"Not only was the assignment a forgery, the collection letter was a lie, and Prudent collected money from Mr. and Mrs. Marsh under false pretenses, isn't that true?"

"Objection, argumentative!" said Stein.

"Sustained!"

"Ms. Gioriano, after your letter, do the collection records show payments made by Mr. and Mrs. Marsh?"

"Yes."

"To Prudent Bank?"

"Yes."

"No further questions, Your Honor."

They used to say in law school, "If the facts are on your side, argue the facts; if the law is on your side, argue the law; and if you have neither on your side, blow smoke." Stein had a difficult time rehabilitating this witness, because the ink had been dry on the documents for so long, but his undeniable skills and experience in blowing smoke lessened the blow of her testimony on the jury.

39

Brent's next witness was Judy Solomon, the notary who had allegedly signed the assignment of the Marsh loan to the trust. She was the teacher type, in her late 40's to early 50's, with tortoise shell glasses over topaz eyes, black straight leg slacks and a white oxford shirt. She appeared to be very likeable, which was not good for Brent.

"Ms. Solomon, you are a notary public for the state of Minnesota, is that correct?"

"Yes I am."

"Calling your attention to Exhibit 5, can you identify the notary stamp on this assignment?"

"It looks like my stamp."

"How about the signature, can you identify that?"

"Well, as a notary for Prudent Bank, I sign my name thousands of times."

"Please answer the question, Ms. Solomon, can you identify the signature?"

"Well, it looks like it could be mine."

"Are you not sure if it's yours?"

"Well, I sign my name so many times, you know? It looks like mine, but I'm not sure."

"Do you remember signing this document?"

"I can't say that I do, no. I sign so many of these."

"Your Honor, may I?"

"Please proceed, Mr. Marks."

Brent put the exhibit on the overhead projector, and it projected a large image on half of the screen adjacent to the jury box. He handed Solomon a blank piece of paper.

"Ms. Solomon, would you please sign your name ten times on this blank piece of paper?"

"Objection, Your Honor, lack of foundation!" barked Stein.

"This is demonstrative, Your Honor. I have not moved its admission."

"Overruled."

Solomon signed her name ten times, and Brent put it on the screen next to the notarized signature.   The signatures obviously did not match.

"What do you say now, Ms. Solomon? Is this your signature?"

"I'm still not sure," said Solomon.

"Ms. Solomon, did you authorize anyone at Prudent Bank or Tentane Mutual to sign your name and use your notary stamp?"

"Why no, that would be illegal."

"And you mentioned before that you signed a lot of documents for Prudent Bank. Were you employed by Prudent Bank at the time this document was signed?"

"Yes I was."

"This is an assignment to the trust pool created by Tentane Mutual in 2006. Why did you notarize this assignment transfer the day after Prudent took over Tentane Mutual?"

"Objection!" said Stein, lack of foundation, argumentative."

"Sustained."

Stein had coached Solomon well. Not only was she unable to express that the document contained a forgery of her signature, she waited for the objection to be ruled on before she answered. But the jury had already heard the question, and you could bet that they would be wondering why a Prudent Bank notary would be notarizing an assignment by Tentane Mutual after the takeover.

Neither Stein nor Black had any questions for this witness, and she was excused. The morning had been productive; full of victories and losses that would mean nothing unless the jury processed them correctly. Brent had noticed some of them nodding off, trying to fight the fact that their brains, sensing boredom, had hit the "hibernate" switch. The judge had called for a lunch break just in time.

40

Michael Shermer, in his book, *The Believing Brain,* pointed out that human brains are "belief engines," designed to recognize patterns and create meaning out of them. Brent knew that once a belief had formed in the minds of the jury about the case, no amount of evidence or argument could shake the jury from that belief, and the fact that they would later deliberate and discuss their beliefs would reinforce similar beliefs of the other jurors.

Brent used the break to turn over Solomon's original signature samples to his handwriting expert, Dr. Albert Dutoit, who took the signature samples from the demonstration back to his lab to examine them. Dutoit was a board certified forensic document examiner, with a Masters in Forensic Science from George Washington University, an M.D. from Stanford, and a charismatic personality. Since the signature on the assignment was obviously not Solomon's, he was probably over qualified for the job. With the precious time Brent had left on the break, he called Angela.

"Don't tell me you're inviting me to lunch?" she quipped.

"No time, I just wanted to know if we had a match on that hair sample from the bar yet."

"Not yet. How's it going?"

"To early to tell. I'm hanging in."

"Well keep hanging."

Brent also checked in with Jack Ruder for an update. The District Attorney had decided to move forward with prosecuting Joshua Banks for the attack on Brent, citing the strength of his confession and the lack of any other suspects. Brent knew their case was hollow as an empty bottle.

41

After the break, Dutoit took the witness stand, and Brent spent a great deal of time going over his qualifications and accolades. Dutoit ran his own forensic lab and had testified as a handwriting expert in countless trials. Brent knew that Stein would not even attempt to challenge his expert, but this show was more important to put on for the jury than anything else. Since it was his most important piece of evidence, Brent had to make sure that the bell rang in each of the twelve's heads and that it festered in them like an ear worm until they got to the jury room to deliberate.

Dr. Dutoit's electric personality put the jurors at ease immediately and he talked to them as if they were guests in his own home, in front of the fireplace drinking hot cocoa. In fact, when he testified, he didn't address Brent with the answer to his questions. He trained his cloud gray eyes straight at the jurors, as if he were sharing with them a well-kept secret. Then Brent touched on the juiciest part; the one that Stein was sure to capitalize on.

"Dr. Dutoit, you were paid to appear here today, isn't that correct?"

"Yes, I was."

"What is your hourly rate?"

"I charge $450 per hour for studies and reports and $600 per hour for court time."

"And have you worked for both plaintiffs and defendants?"

"I have. I've also worked for the prosecution and defense side in numerous criminal cases."

Not missing a beat, Brent moved to the meat of Dr. Dutoit's testimony.

"Dr. Dutoit, when I hired you for this case, I asked you to examine documents that Ms. Solomon had notarized for Prudent Bank, is that correct?"

"Yes."

"What did I ask you to look for?"

"You asked me to look for discrepancies in her signature."

"What documents did you examine?"

"I reviewed and analyzed over 500 documents that were allegedly notarized by Ms. Solomon. There are many elements that go into signature analysis, and I examined and considered them all."

"Can you explain the process of signature analysis and what elements you examined in each signature sample?"

"Certainly. The process of signing one's name is unique to every individual, like a fingerprint. A signature consists of a series of rapid movements, made by the human neuromuscular system. It is essentially a task of pattern recognition.

There are two types of signature analysis; offline, which is the study of the patterns of the genuine signature in comparison to the suspect signature, and online, which involves the use of special software that has been developed to evaluate not only the contours but the movements made to create a signature."

"Doctor, can you explain this in layman's terms?"

"Of course. It would be easier to demonstrate. May I?"

"Yes."

Dutoit put the demonstration samples of Solomon's signature on the overhead and went through them with his pointer.

"Here are the signature samples taken this morning from the witness, Judy Solomon. Every genuine signature will vary from one to another, but a trained eye looks for patterns in the genuine signature that are always the same; such as the height and width of the signature, here," said Dutoit, pointing at the examples. "You can see that these signatures are all about the same height and width even though they may vary in size.

"We also look at the slant and angle of the signature, and you can see that there is the same basic slant and angle pattern with each one of these examples, even though they vary in total size. We also look for horizontal and vertical peaks, like these here, and differences in baseline shift between the vertical centers of gravity as I am pointing out on these examples, between the left and the right part of the signature image, the number of cross points, which are these, and the number of closed loops, which you can see here."

"Then, after looking at the images, we grid them, as you can see that I have done in this slide," he said, putting a grid overlay slide over the signature samples.

"In the grid, each image is divided into 96 rectangular regions, and we look for the patterns and compare them with each image example. As you can see, with these images signed by Ms. Solomon today, they essentially match each other."

"Finally, we use an online analysis with special software, which measures speed, acceleration, curvature, and signature pressure." Dutoit put up another slide, showing Solomon's signature as analyzed online. "These are a series of signatures that Ms. Solomon performed in her deposition. We scanned in her alleged signatures from the public records as well as the signature on the assignment for comparison."

"As a result of your analysis of Ms. Solomon's signature, and comparison with the 500 signatures you examined from the public record, as well as the signature on the assignment, what conclusions did you come to?"

"I compared the signatures on the public records with signatures that Ms. Solomon provided to you in deposition, and analyzed them in comparison to each other. Out of the 500 documents I examined, only one hundred three of them contained…"

"Objection!" said Stein. "Irrelevant."

"Counsel, please approach the bench," said Judge Masters.

"Your Honor, it is highly prejudicial to compare signatures on other documents when we should be focusing on the one that is relevant to this case," argued Stein.

"Your Honor, this shows a pattern of forgery and fraud that is consistent in this case, and is relevant to the RICO count to show a criminal enterprise," Brent argued.

"That is a good point, Mr. Marks, but I agree with Mr. Stein that its prejudicial impact far outweighs any probative value. I am not going to allow any further discussion of anything other than a signature comparison of the Exhibits."

After Brent, Stein and Black took their positions at counsel table, Judge Masters instructed, "Ladies and Gentlemen of the jury, you are instructed to disregard any testimony regarding signatures of Ms. Solomon on any other documents. The only document that contains her signature that is relevant in this case is Exhibit 5 and the signature samples that she signed in court. You may proceed, Mr. Marks."

"Dr. Dutoit, did you examine and compare the signature on Exhibit 5 with Ms. Solomon's signature samples?"

"Yes, I did."

"And what conclusions, if any, did you come to?"

"The signature on Exhibit 5, the assignment, is a forgery."

"How so?"

"It is what is known as a random forgery. With a simulated skilled forgery, the forger attempts to imitate the genuine signature by looking at it, tracing it, or duplicating it as closely as possible. This is a random forgery, because it fits none of the patterns of the genuine signature. A random forgery is a forgery made by a person who has absolutely no information about the genuine signer's signature. This forgery was made by someone who was not even attempting to imitate the genuine signature."

"And how do you know that?"

"If the forger had referred to a copy of the original signature, he or she would have tried to simulate the genuine signature in some way; we call this a simple simulated signature. May I show you?"

"Yes." Dutoit put up a slide of the original signature and Exhibit 5.

"This is the original signature. First of all, the overall size of the image is smaller. Secondly, the loops are completely different in each of the o's, and l's" he said, pointing to them with his pointer. "Now, when I overlay the grid, you can see what I mean in measured space. As you can see here, the "S" in "Solomon" in the original is looped– always– and the "S" in Exhibit 5 bears no loop. The curvature, here, and the slant, here, are completely different."

"So, in terms of percentage, what is your belief that Exhibit 5 is a forgery?"

"I am 100% sure that the signature on Exhibit 5 is made by a different person than Ms. Solomon and that it is a forgery."

"Thank you, Your Honor, no further questions."

"Mr. Stein, your witness."

"Thank you, Your Honor. Dr. Dutoit, isn't it true that, when one signs one's signature, it does not appear exactly the same every time?"

"Yes, that's true. It will always be a little different, but…"

"Move to strike after 'yes' Your Honor."

"Granted."

"And isn't it also true that the signature samples you analyzed from Ms. Solomon's deposition were made on a special pad that performs more functions that a mere scan of a two dimensional signature?"

"Yes, but…"

"Move to strike after 'yes' Your Honor."

"Granted."

Stein continued on with his cross examination of Dutoit on obvious points, but failed to make a dent in his armor. Brent had a few follow up questions on redirect, but the damage to Prudent Bank had already been done. It was clear that the assignment was not only done late, it was also a forgery. Prudent Bank was clearly in Brent's cross-hairs at the end of this first day of trial.

42

Brent dragged his body home after the long drive on the saturated freeways from Los Angeles at travel time, exhausted, and poured himself through the front door, spilling the pile of unopened mail he had from the mailbox onto the floor of the entry. Calico swarmed around his legs and mewed for her dinner.

"Okay baby, I know you're hungry. Let's go."

The kitty dutifully followed Brent into the kitchen, then ran ahead of him to her empty bowl, which Brent filled with a generous packet of saucy cat food. Then he went to the bedroom, peeled off and hung his suit and basked in the warmth of a rejuvenating and relaxing shower.

Brent's mind was going 600 miles an hour as he tried to force himself to think about something other than the trial. It was practically impossible to do, so he put on some jazz music to try to calm himself down.

He fixed himself a Baileys on the rocks, and sat at the kitchen table, looking out over the Santa Barbara harbor and going over his trial notes for the next day, when, suddenly, the doorbell rang.

Brent did not desire any unwanted visitors, such as the "Mike" character from Carl's Junior, or any visitors at all for that matter. However, he quickly changed his mind when he looked through the peep-hole. Brent opened the door to the smiling face of Angela, who was holding a bottle of champagne in one hand and a bottle of massage oil in the other.

"I thought you could use some relaxation therapy," she said, as Brent ushered her in.

"I couldn't think of anything better."

"Just go into the bedroom, relax, and let me do everything," she said, as Brent happily complied.

Moments later, Angela entered the room with champagne on ice, stripped down to her black, lacy underwear, and began a delightful, relaxing massage that Brent never could have dreamed of.

"Have you forgotten about work yet?"

"Almost."

"Well then, I have a sure fire remedy to make you forget right away."

Angela's palms massaged Brent from his chest, and she moved painfully slowly down his torso, tickling every nerve of his skin until it was obvious what her secret remedy was.

43

Brent had prepared April well for her testimony. Since her father would not be present at trial, it would provide the emotional background needed to evoke sympathy from the jury.

April went on the stand, dressed well but conservatively, as usual, in her best blue silk blouson. She painfully and tearfully described the night she found her mother murdered, and her father gasping within the last inches of his life. It was a harrowing and gruesome description that Brent listened to with sympathetic eyes, diverting his glance from April to share his emotions with the jury from time to time. Twenty four other sad and shocked eyes fixated on April as she testified. After the sad stage had been set, Brent continued to question her to lay the foundation for bringing Jack Ruder to the stand.

"Ms. Marsh, did you perform a full inventory of all the valuable items in your parents' home after the attack?"

"Yes, I did."

"And what was the result of your inventory?"

"Nothing was missing."

"Were you aware of the financial difficulties your father had been experiencing around the time of the attack?"

"Objection, calls for speculation," said Stein.

"Join," said Black.

"Your Honor, I'm just asking if she was aware."

"Overruled. You may answer the question, Ms. Marsh."

"Yes, I was aware that Dad had lost a great deal of his portfolio in the stock crash, and was without cash flow to manage his business."

"How were you aware of this?"

"Because he asked me for a loan to help him get through until the financing closed."

"Were you surprised by this request?"

"Yes."

"Why?"

"Because Dad's business had always been successful. He'd even gone into semi-retirement and had been living off his investments."

"You mentioned a financing. What financing?"

"He had taken a loan out on the house with Tentane Mutual."

"Objection, hearsay," said Stein.

"Counsel, please approach the bench."

Once at the bench, the judge queried Brent, "Why is this not hearsay, Mr. Marks?"

"Your Honor, the fact of the loan is already in evidence. I am laying a foundation for the next witness, not trying to use her testimony as proof that Mr. Marsh took out the loan."

"Objection overruled."

"So, your father asked you for a loan. Then what did you do?"

"I told him I could help, of course, but I asked if I could take a look at his books and records to see if what he was asking me for would tide him over until the loan closed."

"Did he show you his books?"

"Yes."

"Did looking at the books affect your decision in any way?"

"Yes."

"How?"

"Dad had been scaling down on his business, and using some retirement income to supplement their living expenses."

"How did this affect your decision?"

"He hadn't asked me for enough money, and the amount that he needed was more than I could give."

"How was that?"

"Well, it seemed to me that what he was asking me for was not enough, as there was not enough income to sustain payments on the loan after it did close."

"Then what happened?"

"I gave him a loan of $20,000."

"Did he ever pay you back?"

"No."

"Ms. Marsh, you are executor of your father's estate, is that correct?"

"Yes."

"Can you please identify what has been marked as Exhibit 14?"

"This is the accounting of the estate, filed with the probate court."

"What assets, if any, did your father have in his estate?"

"Just the house. That was his only remaining asset."

"Thank you, Ms. Marsh."

Neither Stein nor Black opted to cross examine April. Repetition of the Marshes' poor financial situation was bad for their case, and they wanted the murder scene to fade as much as possible from the jury's memory.

44

The next important witness would be George Marsh, speaking from the grave, but on trial would be augmentative and alternative communication, and Dr. Beverly Senlon would set the stage for playing George Marsh's video-taped testimony. Dr. Senlon was dressed demurely but attractively and spoke well to the jury, as if they were attending a consultation in her office.

"Dr. Senlon, can you please give the Court a brief summary of your professional background?" asked Brent.

"I completed my undergraduate studies in psychology at UCLA and went on to their graduate studies program, eventually receiving a PhD in clinical and forensic psychology."

"Have you testified as an expert in court before?"

"Yes, I have."

"About how many times?"

"I'd say more than ten times."

"And can you describe your current professional occupation, please?"

"I have a practice which specializes in speech pathology, providing solutions for people in need of augmentative and alternative communication."

"Have you published any papers on the subject of your specialty?"

"Yes, I have written several research papers that were published in *the American Medical Journal*, as well as many articles in *Psychology Today*.

"I am showing you a document marked as Exhibit 15. Can you identify this document?"

"It's my curriculum vitae, which lists all of my education, experience, publications, and professional associations I belong to."

Brent moved Exhibit 15 into evidence and tendered Dr. Senlon as an expert witness, and both Stein and Black waived voir dire to test her qualifications.

"Can you describe what augmentative and alternative communication is, please?"

"Yes.   Augmentative and alternative communication, or AAC, is a description for methods used to supplement or replace speech or writing for those with impairments in the production or comprehension of spoken or written language. It's used by people who have a wide range of speech and language impairments, caused by any number of impairments, such as cerebral palsy, autism, ALS and Parkinson's disease."

"And how exactly is AAC used?"

"It can vary, depending on the severity of the speech impediment. If a patient has the ability to make some sounds to communicate, they are encouraged to do so, even with the use of a speech generating device. We can incorporate sign language and body language, facial expressions, or even picture boards or spelling boards, depending on the patient's motor, visual, cognitive, language and communication strengths and weaknesses. We essentially design a customized communication system for each particular patient. It's kind of like learning a new language."

As Dr. Senlon testified, Brent checked the jury box to ascertain if any of the jurors seemed to be lost in technical confusion or boredom. All of them seemed to be relatively alert and there were no puzzled or frustrated looks on their faces.

"Was George Marsh one of your patients in need of AAC?"

245

"He was."

"What type of a system, if any, did you design for Mr. Marsh?"

"I designed an alternative communication system that consists of an electronic tablet application for a communication board, which requires the use of an interpreter familiar with the system. Each family member or friend of Mr. Marsh would have had to learn the system in order to communicate with him."

Senlon next described her app with the aid of the overhead projector. So far, no jury members appeared to be lost; they even looked interested.

"Mr. Marsh had been so incapacitated from the injuries he sustained in the attack, that the only part of his body he could move was his eyes. He had no ability to make any facial expressions, so I had to design a system of communication using symbols that he could point to with his eye movements. This required training on the part of Mr. Marsh as to which symbols to point to, and whomever would interpret what he was saying, which was initially going to be me."

"Dr. Senlon, were you present during the deposition of George Marsh in this case?"

"I was."

"And did you interpret Mr. Marsh's communications for the court reporter with the use of the system you have just described?"

"I did."

Brent completed his questioning of Dr. Senlon, and it was time to feed her to the sharks for cross-examination.

"Dr. Senlon," asked Joe Stein, "As a speech pathologist, you're familiar with American Sign Language, are you not?"

"Yes, I am."

"And isn't it true that American Sign Language is an alternative language to speaking that is standardized; meaning each symbol used will mean exactly the same thing to any person who sees it?"

"Yes."

"Isn't it also true, Dr. Senlon, that augmentative and alternative communication is not a standardized form of communication?"

"Objection," said Brent, "Argumentative."

"Overruled, you may answer."

"I don't understand the question."

"Isn't it true, Dr. Senlon, that the symbols used for augmentative and alternative communication are different from patient to patient; they are not standardized like the gestures in American Sign Language are?"

"Yes, that is true."

"So, it also stands to reason, does it not, that your interpretation of Mr. Marsh's testimony really cannot be verified by anyone except for you, isn't that correct?"

"At this point, yes."

"So then, by interpreting for Mr. Marsh, you are asking the jury to accept your *opinion* as to what he is trying to communicate to you, isn't that so?"

"Objection!" said Brent, "Argumentative."

"Sustained."

* * *

Brent next asked the judge for permission to present the video-taped deposition of George Marsh. The judge agreed, and instructed the jury as to what a deposition was, and how the video tape would be used in Court. It was accompanied by the written transcript of the deposition for each juror to follow. The predicate act of murder hung on the last sentence that George Marsh composed in the deposition, *"It was him!"* and that was not what anyone would call a solid piece of testimony. Nevertheless, it was the only shot they had, so Brent paid close attention to the jury when the last of the tape was played.

It was a message from the past. Hopefully, the jury could formulate some kind of a feeling for the man, who was now just an image on the television screen. The man who had been a loving husband, a strong father. The man whose life had been destroyed in the name of greed. It was the dry and cold message from the grave that closed the second day of the trial of Marsh v. Prudent Bank.

45

Detective William Branson was the next witness to take the stage. He dutifully outlined the crime scene and showed the gruesome photographs.

He testified that the case was never solved, but it was recently reactivated when a private investigator brought forth some possible new evidence that was currently being evaluated in cooperation with the FBI.

"Objection, Your Honor, unfair surprise," said Stein.

"Counsel, please approach."

When all were present at the bench, Stein objected to the mention of new evidence that was being evaluated because it had not been provided to the defense in discovery. The judge asked,

"Mr. Marks, was this witness made available for deposition?"

"Yes, Your Honor."

"Then why are we hearing about this new evidence for the first time at trial?"

"Because it's new evidence, Your Honor. Recent physical evidence that has been obtained is being analyzed for its DNA makeup now, under supervision of the FBI. This witness is not presenting that new evidence."

"Yes, but he's talking about it."

"Your Honor, if you will simply allow me to connect it up later, and, if the new evidence does not materialize, I will stipulate to strike the testimony."

"That's not going to work, Your Honor," said Stein. "The defense is entitled to examine all evidence, so that a defense may be presented."

"I'm afraid Mr. Stein is right, Mr. Marks. I'm going to sustain the objection."

The lawyers took their seats.

"Ladies and Gentlemen of the jury, you will disregard Detective Branson's testimony about possible new evidence being found."

That was another blow to the weakest link in Brent's case. In short order, Stein took over on cross-examination and destroyed Detective Branson.

"Detective Branson, no leads were ever found in this case, isn't that correct?"

"That is correct."

"And isn't it also correct that, with regard to physical evidence, only one hair fiber was found on the scene?"

"Yes, that is correct."

"And there has never been a match found to that hair sample, isn't that correct?"

"No, that is not correct."

"Detective Branson, you just testified that no leads were ever found in the case, correct?"

"Yes, but that is the new evidence. A hair fiber was found in investigator Rick Penn's car after his disappearance and it matches the…"

"Objection Your Honor, we have already discussed this."

"Detective Branson, do you have any personal knowledge about this hair fiber that was found?" asked Judge Masters.

"No, it was found by Agent Wollard of the FBI."

"Objection, Your Honor and move to strike, hearsay and lack of foundation."

"Granted. The jury will disregard this witnesses' testimony regarding any hair fibers found in Mr. Penn's car."

Brent now had no choice. He had to call Angela. Stein continued to wreak havoc on Branson, turning him into more of a witness for the defense, with his acute cross examination skills.

"Detective, you never had the chance to interview the surviving victim, Mr. Marsh, isn't that correct?"

"No I didn't. He was in a coma after the incident."

"But even after he came out of the coma, you never had the chance to interview him, isn't that so?"

"Yes."

"In fact, you tried to interview him, didn't you?"

"Yes, several times."

"And he was unresponsive to your questions every time, isn't that correct?"

"Yes."

"He was uncommunicative?"

"Yes."

"In fact, he didn't seem at all coherent to you, did he?"

"No."

"And, in fact, you had the impression that he wasn't even aware that you were speaking to him, isn't that true?"

"Objection!" declared Brent, "Lack of foundation. Detective Branson is not qualified to diagnose Mr. Marsh's condition."

"Sustained."

"Was Mr. Marsh able to answer yes or no?"

"No."

"Did you notice any movement of his eyes, like he was trying to communicate with you?"

"Same objection, Your Honor," said Brent.

"I'll allow it. Please answer the question."

"No, he seemed completely out of it."

"Objection, lack of foundation and move to strike."

"Overruled."

* * *

For the first time since Brent had met her, Angela looked and spoke like a real G-man on the witness stand. She was dressed in an attractive, but conservative suit, with her hair pinned back in a bun.

"Agent Wollard," asked Brent, "Are you currently investigating the disappearance of my private investigator, Richard Penn?"

"I am."

"And during the course of your investigation, have you obtained any evidence that could be related to the Marsh murder case?"

"Yes. I found a hair fiber in an extensive search of Mr. Penn's car after his disappearance. The hair's DNA matches the hair fiber found at the Marsh murder scene."

"And have you had any progress determining the identity of the person from the hair sample?"

"Not yet. We are currently testing the hair that was uncovered in a private investigation to determine if there is a match."

"What private investigation is that?"

"Yours. The sample was brought in by Jack Ruder, your new investigator."

Stein and Black both objected. "Your Honor, I object to this continued line of questioning that seems to be not connected to anything in this case."

"I will connect it up with the next witness, Your Honor," said Brent.

The judge overruled the objection, and broke for the mid-morning break. Brent left the courtroom with Angela.

"Thanks, Angie."

"Angie? You never called me that before," she said, and smiled with her eyes.

"I guess not. Do you have anything back on the DNA test yet?"

"No, there's a rush on it. It's supposed to be any day now."

"Yeah, but I'm running out of days."

Brent had to think of an alternative strategy to propel this case to a win.

46

It was the third day of the trial. Brent had one more day to present the remainder of his case, which was still based on thin air.

"Come on, Jack, I need a miracle here," said Brent during the lunch break.

"Sorry, Brent, so far we have no results on that DNA test."

"Any leads on George Marsh?"

"The Coroner is calling it death by natural consequences."

"Then we have to ask for an inquest. How about my case?"

"They're still planning to prosecute Banks for it."

"Great."

After a few bites of his lunch, Brent suddenly had an epiphany.

"Jack, can you serve that dirt bag Suskind with a subpoena to have him come to court to testify tomorrow?"

"Yeah, but I'm sure he won't testify. He'll claim the Fifth, most likely."

"Serve him, and make sure he gets to court, even if you have to get him arrested or something."

"Okay, I'll do it."

The rest of the day was uneventful, with Brent putting on less important witnesses, to make sure he got all the documents in so he could show the time line to the jury during his argument.

The timeline showed a pattern of fraud and cover-up from the moment that Prudent had taken over the loan; from its late assignment to the Trust, which was a robo-signed forgery, to the latest assignment to a new trustee who would carry out the foreclosure sale. That part of the case looked pretty solid and formed the basis of the first predicate act of the RICO case. What was not solid was the RICO case. Brent needed to prove one more predicate act: murder.

On the long drive home, Brent planned his next moves in his head. He concocted a surprise attack that Stein and Black could have never foreseen. Although he had no idea what the outcome would be, something had to shake up this case, and this idea definitely would.

It was getting dark when Brent pulled into his driveway on Harbor Hills Drive and parked alongside a government issued white Crown Victoria. Angela was still inside the car, smiling.

"I've got a surprise for you!" she exclaimed as she got out of the car, holding a manila envelope.

The sight of Angela made Brent feel stronger already. He jumped out of the car and gave her a hug.

"Where's my surprise?" he asked.

Angela handed him the manila envelope. "We got the DNA test back today. Kevin Suskind is definitely our man. We can place him at the murder scene and in Rick's car, plus he's one of the guys who followed you. We're going to pick him up in Rick's case tomorrow morning."

"It's fantastic news. Thank you. And Angela…"

"Yes?"

"Be careful."

"Brent, I'm a trained FBI agent. I'll have body armor on and a full team to take this guy down. He'll come without a fight, believe me."

"It's just that…"

"What?"

"I care about you."

"I care about you too Brent. You're the one who needs to be careful. Your job is much more dangerous than mine – especially lately."

They kissed and Angela got in her car and drove off. Brent called Jack to make sure he was standing by. Now there was no doubt that Suskind would be in court tomorrow. And while he may not say a word, he was sure to be the most important witness that Brent would ever call in the case of Marsh v. Prudent Bank.

47

Jack Ruder was dressed in the blue uniform of a FedEx driver when he knocked on Kevin Suskind's door. In his left hand was a FedEx overnight envelope, and the right hand rested on the handle of his concealed .38 snub nose revolver. He rang the doorbell and waited.

"Who is it?" an annoyed voice from inside the house asked, through the door.

"FedEx," said Jack, and smiled for the peephole.

"I ain't expecting no FedEx," said the voice.

"I have urgent business correspondence here addressed to a Kevin Suskind at this address."

The door opened a crack. The fat meathead from the biker bar looked out at Jack.

"Kevin Suskind?" Jack smiled again, holding out an electronic clipboard for a signature.

"Yeah, it's me."

As Suskind signed the clipboard, Jack handed him the envelope and said,

"Kevin Suskind, you are served."

Suskind threw the envelope and the clipboard back at Jack and slammed the door.

"Your failure to appear as a witness will result in a warrant for your arrest," Jack said, through the door.

"Eat me," said Suskind.

* * *

"Well, that went well," Brent said, as Jack relayed the details of the service. "But don't worry, the FBI is picking him up tomorrow morning. Make sure they have the subpoena and we'll have our sneaky little scumbag on deck for tomorrow."

Brent worked that evening on restructuring his trial strategy. He had one and only one shot at making RICO stick in the minds of the jury, and that was to prove that it was more likely than not that Bernstein was responsible for the attack on April's parents.

True to the character of the paranoid crack head that he was, Suskind spent his evening getting high and looking out his window for more process servers, or, in the case of every drug addict's obsession, the cops. The pent up adrenaline in his blood was urging him to action and he could not sit still.

As he got more and more stoked up, supercharged by the increase in his heartbeat, Suskind reached that point where he felt driven by a mystical dark energy that took control over his mind and body. Like Mr. Hyde, he was transformed.

48

Four government issued Crown Victorias pulled up to the small house of Kevin Suskind, in the "Mexican" area of Santa Barbara. Eight agents, including Angela Wollard, all dressed in "Ninja" gear – body armor under windbreakers which bore the insignia "FBI" in yellow letters on the back – exited the cars in almost a synchronized motion, and each agent took up a strategic position at certain points in front, on the side and in back of the house.

Angela, with her weapon drawn, approached the front door with a fellow agent, Dave Edwards. Each of them moved to each side of the door as Angela rapped on it.

"FBI!" she called out.

Not a sound could be heard from inside the run down bungalow.

"FBI!" Angela shouted again, knocking loudly on the door.

Suddenly, a loud crack – the sound of a car breaking through the aluminum garage door – gave way to the smoking, screeching tires of Suskind's white 2006 Ford Mustang GT, which flew backwards out the garage, and smashed the back of one Crown Victoria as it turned, spinning like a top. The Mustang accelerated down San Andres Street, leaving a cloud of rubber seared smoke behind it.

"Suspect fleeing arrest scene in a 2006 white Ford Mustang, California license plate BGB FN3," yelled Angela into her shoulder radio, as she jumped behind the wheel of one of the Crown Victorias. Edwards jumped in the passenger side to ride shotgun as the car sped off.

"Agent Wollard, suspect vehicle spotted by SBPD heading north on Highway 101 at Las Positas Road at high speed," a voice crackled over the government frequency.

"Copy that, we are in pursuit," said Angela, as she flew the Crown Vic up the freeway onramp.

"There he is!" exclaimed Edwards.

Just ahead, they saw the white Mustang weaving in and out of traffic. It was pursued by a black and white SBPD patrol car.

"Call CHP and advise that we are in a high speed pursuit northbound 101; ask them to clear the freeway at Patterson Road," Angela advised.

The Mustang swerved left on the left shoulder to get around a white Toyota Corolla in the number one lane, and bounced off the concrete barrier, and back into the Toyota, sending it spinning. Angela continued pursuit, avoiding the Toyota, which hit the divider, and came to an abrupt stop. Two CHP black and whites charged up the onramp ahead at Patterson, lights blazing like the Las Vegas strip.

As the Mustang accelerated, Angela passed the pursuing SBPD squad car. "What are you doing?" asked Edwards.

"As soon as he drops his speed, I'm going to PIT him," she replied.

"What if he doesn't?"

Angela pushed the Victoria even further, slamming her foot down on the gas pedal and wiping beads of nervous sweat from her forehead. If the PIT maneuver was successful, it would disable the Mustang. If not, it could result in disaster, killing not only Suskind, but her and Edwards as well.

"CHP, this is Agent Wollard. I am going to attempt to PIT the suspect vehicle; request assistance."

"Angela, let CHP do it. They have the experience."

The two CHP units began a controlled weave ahead, slowing methodically as the speeding pack approached.

Angela gained on the Mustang as its speed decreased a bit, and pulled alongside the rear of it. Suskind swung his head back to look and panicked, swerving to the right just as Angela pushed right into the rear of the Mustang, forcing the back of it to the right as well, sending it into a skid. The searing sound of screeching metal and burning rubber was all she could hear as the tarred smoke filled the interior of the Victoria, which flew into an uncontrolled spin itself.

As Suskind struggled to recover from the skid, the two CHP units attempted to box him in. Suskind, in his drug induced panic, turned against the spin and the Mustang began doing 360's, finally landing in some bushes on the right shoulder.

In the Victoria, time seemed to go in slow motion. Angela steered in the direction of the spin at first, eased off, then straightened out, and eased off again until they came to a soft landing next to the Mustang.

Suskind jumped out the passenger side and ran into the brush, with two CHP officers and Angela in hot pursuit.

49

"The Plaintiff calls Steven Bernstein as an adverse witness," Brent said, with his eyes on the jury.

Bernstein took a seat in the witness box to begin his ordeal. It was a "winner take all" match. In order to have a chance to win the RICO case, Brent had two impossible tasks; he had to prove that it was more likely than not that Bernstein had committed or aided and abetted a murder; and, even more difficult, that he had done it within the scope of his employment at Prudent Bank as part of the fraud cover-up. It may have been easier for Brent to produce a diamond from a lump of coal before the jury's eyes, but he was going to give it his best shot. And, if the moon and the stars lined up properly, he had a secret weapon.

"Mr. Bernstein, you are the current Vice President in charge of the real estate loan department at Prudent Bank since September 26, 2008, is that correct?"

"Yes, I am."

"And immediately before taking that position, you were the executive manager of Tentane Mutual Bank in Santa Barbara, is that correct?"

"Yes."

Brent could see that the jury was already making their shoulder pillows ready for a long nap during his preliminary questioning, so he threw in a wake-up bomb.

"Mr. Bernstein, shortly after your appointment as Vice President of Prudent Bank, you were served with a subpoena in a Grand Jury investigation of alleged bank fraud involving Prudent Bank and Tentane Mutual, is that correct?"

"Objection!" said Stein.

At the bench, the judge ruled in Brent's favor, giving Brent the opportunity to repeat the question for emphasis.

"Mr. Bernstein, you are aware, are you not, that you have a privilege against self-incrimination…"

"Objection!" yelled Stein.

"….And that you are not compelled to answer any questions that may tend to incriminate you…"

"Objection!" said Black.

"Counsel, approach the bench!" said the judge.

"Mr. Marks, I will not have you turn my courtroom into a cheap theater, is that understood?"

"Yes, Your Honor."

"I hope so, now let us continue the questioning without any more theatrics, shall we?"

The judge sustained the objection, and cautioned the jury to disregard it, which, of course, was impossible. Brent continued.

"Mr. Bernstein, shortly after your appointment as Vice President of Prudent Bank, you were served with a subpoena in a Grand Jury investigation of an alleged bank fraud involving Prudent Bank and Tentane Mutual, is that correct?"

"You may answer the question, Mr. Bernstein," said the judge.

"Yes, I was."

"And you came to understand that the principal witness against your employer in this

Grand Jury investigation was George Marsh, isn't that correct?"

"Objection!" said Stein and Black, simultaneously.

"Overruled, the witness may answer if that was his understanding or not," said the judge.

"I understood that he was a witness," said Bernstein.

"You had a meeting with Marsh, where he asked for a refinance of the loan on his property, is that correct?"

"We discussed that, yes."

"And you told Mr. Marsh at that time that a refinance was impossible, did you not?"

"I did."

Every teacher of cross-examination points out that you never ask a question that you do not know the answer to, and you never ask the question "why" because that gives the witness the opportunity to answer in a narrative, but Brent wanted the jury to hear the answer to the next question in Bernstein's own words, so he took the calculated risk.

"Why was it impossible?"

"Because Mr. Marsh was delinquent in his loan payments."

"But Mr. Bernstein, didn't you tell Mr. Marsh about six months earlier that, in order to qualify for a loan modification, he had to be delinquent in his loan payments?"

"That's for a modification, not a refinance, and that was Tentane's policy…"

"Object and move to strike," said Stein, "argumentative."

"Overruled. Please finish your answer, Mr. Bernstein," said the judge.

"Tentane Mutual's policy was not to consider any loan modification unless the borrower was delinquent in their payments. I told Mr. Marsh at the time that it may be easier for him to qualify for a loan modification than a refinance, because the qualification criteria was relaxed. But it was his decision."

"But you didn't tell Mr. Marsh at that time that falling behind in his mortgage payments would disqualify him from refinancing his home equity loan, isn't that correct?"

"It was a different company and a different criteria…"

"Move to strike as non-responsive, Your Honor," said Brent.

"Granted. Answer the question, Mr. Bernstein."

"No, I didn't."

When he left the courtroom, Brent grabbed Jack by the elbow.

"Any word on Suskind yet?"

"Nothing."

"Get on it, man, this is the last day I've got."

Brent left for the morning break with the bases loaded and plenty of innings left to go in the game. But he was still a long way from getting enough evidence in front of the jury, and still holding out for a miracle.

50

Angela Wollard was not only the top of her class at Quantico during her 20 weeks of FBI training, she was also the top sprinter, which topped off a long series of trophies beginning in her childhood and finishing in college. As Kevin Suskind's cocaine powered frantic getaway run propelled his fat body across the urban obstacle course over walls, in backyards and through the brush, she was, at times, so close to him she could hear him pant as she held the lead in the chase.

Suskind ran for his life. Escape was his only option, and he had nothing to lose. He had no idea what the FBI had on him, but he was certain that it was enough to put him behind bars for life. As he ran, he thought of nothing but running faster and finding a place to hole out until he could be whisked out of the country to safety.

As Suskind reached the fenced end of a dead end alley, Angela knew she had him. Suskind leaped onto the fence like a tree frog, scrambling up the mesh as Angela flew at him, missing his legs by inches. He scrambled over the top of the fence and jumped down and Angela hopped down after him, almost landing on him. Suskind regained his balance and ran through the vacant field, as the two CHP officers scurried over the fence, taking up the rear of the pursuit.

Angela ran so close to Suskind, she could hear the ruffling of his shirt and see the sweat on his neck. Calculating her last move, she tackled him around his knees, bringing him down, but in his drug powered, testosterone fueled strength, he dragged her through the dirt and broke loose.

As Angela stood, Suskind whirled around and pulled his .38 revolver from its hidden holster and pointed it at Angela. The loud, cannon-like boom was the last thing she heard as her body hit the dirt.

"Officer down!" screamed one CHP into his shoulder mike, as he felt for a pulse and his partner continued the pursuit.

51

"Damn it, where is Suskind?" asked Brent, pulling Jack aside during the break.

"Brent, I've got some bad news."

Brent listened somberly as Jack told him what he knew so far; that Angela had been shot in the pursuit, and Suskind was still being pursued. Brent's whole world came crushing down in that instant. What seemed to always be clear was not anymore. What seemed to be important before was inconsequential.

"Is she alright...is she alive?"

"She's alive, on her way to the hospital in an ambulance. But we won't know anything else until she sees the emergency doctors."

"I've got to leave, have to ask for a recess."

After the short afternoon break, Brent approached the bench to ask for a recess.

"Your request for a recess is denied, Mr. Marks."

"But, Your Honor…"

"I understand your urgency, but, as I told you before, the time for trial has been set and it will not be altered."

Nothing would tame the cold heart of Judge Masters. Not life or death, or even a near death crisis would convince her to bend her own rules

"Mr. Bernstein," instructed the judge, "you will take your position in the witness box. Mr. Marks, please continue."

Brent felt buried alive, suffocated. He couldn't think about anything, only thoughts of Angela lying on the ground, shot, bleeding. That image came to him with every thought, and the anxiety was gnawing at his brain. He couldn't leave the courtroom, and there was nothing he could do at the moment to help Angela.

Since the crisis of 2008, the big banks had been bailed out by the government; the tax payers stuck with the bill. Prudent Bank had been able to foreclose on Tentane Mutual's properties, and had collected on its bad debts, to the tune of billions more than it had paid for them. The wealth of the United States had been redistributed; the middle class transformed into the "lower middle class." It was time for someone to pay.

Suddenly, a surge of anger overcame him like a wave of power. He pointed that wave at Bernstein and let him have it.

"Mr. Bernstein, before the break, you testified that you didn't tell Mr. Marsh that falling behind in his mortgage payments would make it impossible for him to refinance his property."

"Not impossible, just more difficult."

"And you didn't tell him that his loan and deed of trust were not assigned to the Trust before the closing of the Pooling Service Agreement, is that correct?"

"He wasn't a party to that agreement."

"Move to strike as non-responsive."

"Granted, answer the question, Mr. Bernstein."

"No, I didn't."

"And you spoke to Mr. Marsh after he received this letter from Prudent Bank to make his further payments to Prudent, didn't you?"

"Yes."

"And, at the time, you discussed the Grand Jury investigation with him, didn't you?"

"I may have mentioned it."

"You may have mentioned it. Wasn't that your very purpose in going to see Mr. Marsh that day?"

"Objection!"

"Overruled."

"No."

"In fact, Mr. Bernstein, you found out about the Grand Jury investigation, a secret proceeding, from your superiors at Prudent Bank, didn't you?"

"I don't remember who told me."

"And you knew that the Bank was being investigated for covering up forged documents..."

"Objection, Your Honor, assumes facts not in evidence."

"...fraudulent transfers, like the assignment of Mr. Marsh's loan to the trust..."

"Objection! Argumentative!"

"Sustained! Mr. Marks! The jury will disregard the question."

"Shall the jury disregard the truth, Your Honor?"

"Counsel, approach the bench!"

Brent was hot, and had no intention of cooling down.

"Mr. Marks, you will obey protocol in my courtroom or I will hold you in contempt, and you'll be spending the night in jail."

"Yes, Your Honor."

Back at counsel table, Brent continued on his roll.

"You knew of the Grand Jury Investigation, didn't you?"

"Yes."

"And you found out about the investigation from Prudent Bank."

"I don't recall."

"And you went to Mr. Marsh because you knew he was a witness in the investigation, isn't that correct?"

"No."

"You discussed the investigation with Mr. Marsh?"

"I may have."

"And you told him not to testify, isn't that true?"

"No."

"You told him that if he testified, he would regret it, didn't you?"

"I said no such thing."

Bernstein was wiggling in his chair, avoiding eye contact and avoiding the jury.

"Are you alright, Mr. Bernstein?"

"Objection, Your Honor."

"Sustained. Mr. Marks, stick to the facts please."

"You discussed your conversation with Mr. Marsh with your superiors at Prudent Bank, isn't that true?"

"I may have; I don't recall."

"Who did you discuss it with?"

"I don't remember."

"Who was your immediate supervisor at the time?"

"Joel Simon."

"And you discussed Mr. Marsh with Mr. Simon?"

"I don't recall."

"You told your superiors at the bank that Mr. Marsh intended to witness against the bank in the Grand Jury investigation, didn't you?"

"I don't recall."

"Mr. Bernstein, after you came back to Prudent Bank, after seeing Mr. Marsh, and after having 'possibly' discussed your conversation with your superiors at the bank, a decision was made to prevent Mr. Marsh from testifying, isn't that true?"

"No."

"And you were charged with implementing that decision, isn't that correct?"

"Objection, Your Honor, lack of foundation."

"Sustained."

"Mr. Bernstein, you ordered the murder of Mr. and Mrs. Marsh, didn't you?"

"No!"

Bernstein was squirming in his chair, blinking incessantly.

"And Prudent Bank knew about it?"

"Objection, lack of foundation, assumes facts not in evidence."

"Sustained.   The jury will disregard the question."

"Mr. Bernstein, you hired two men to murder Mr. and Mrs. Marsh, didn't you?"

"No!"

Bernstein scratched his nose.   He tugged at his collar.

"You were there at the time of the attack, weren't you?"

"No!"

"You know who beat the life out of Mrs. Marsh, don't you Mr. Bernstein?"

"No! That's ridiculous!"

"And you know who killed Mr. Marsh in the hospital, don't you?"

"Objection, lack of foundation!" Stein boomed.

"Sustained."

"And you know who is responsible for the murder of my investigator on this case, Rick Penn, don't you?"

"Objection, assumes facts not in evidence."

"Sustained. Counsel, please approach."

By the time they broke for lunch, Brent had been admonished by the judge countless times for improper grandstanding before the jury. If the secret weapon he had in mind materialized, he may be spending the night in a jail cell. But the only thing on his mind right now was Angela and, trial or no trial, he headed straight for the hospital.

52

Kevin Suskind, powered by paranoia and fueled by cocaine, was freaking out that he had shot an FBI agent. He couldn't afford to stop running and being caught was not an option. He jumped another fence into a backyard, but the CHP officer was still hot on his tail. He jumped out of the yard into another, and another, but this strategy just seemed to slow the entire process down. He needed to break free of his pursuer, long enough to make a call and be picked up and taken to a safe house.

On the next jump, Suskind twisted his ankle on the landing in the soft rows of a broccoli farm, but his high and the need to escape dulled his pain. Nevertheless, it slowed him down.

"Freeze!" said the CHP officer. Suskind turned his head to glance behind him, and found the officer about 50 yards away, in a shooting stance with his weapon drawn.

"Put your hands on your head!" commanded the officer, and Suskind obeyed. The second officer arrived and drew his weapon also, covering his partner. It was over for Suskind. The first officer approached him with his gun trained on him at every second, felt his pockets, disarmed him of his .38, then handcuffed him.

"29 CHP, Highway 101, unit 9, I have WMA suspect in custody, requesting backup," said the officer into his shoulder mic.

* * *

Brent ran into the emergency room in a panic, and was directed to a room where Angela lay, hooked up to an IV. When he entered the room, she smiled.

"Thank God you're alive!"

"I'm fine, just bruises. But look at the vest," she said, pointing to the chair beside her. Brent pulled up Angela's flak jacket by its straps, and could see the bullet holes.

"Five shots, two of them hit me in the chest," she said. Brent hugged Angela.

"You're not going to make me cry," she said, wiping a forming tear from her eye.

"No more playing super cop," he said. She nodded, and squeezed him, wincing from the pain in her ribs.

"They caught the guy," she said. "Now get back to court and fry them!"

53

Back in the courtroom, Steven Bernstein resumed his place in the witness box when court came to order. Judge Masters would not waste a minute of the carefully allocated court time.

"Mr. Bernstein, do you know a Kevin Suskind?"

"Objection, Your Honor, assumes facts not in evidence," said Black, finally chiming in.

At the bench, Black argued, "Your Honor, the name Kevin Suskind has never come up in discovery."

"That's because he's an impeachment witness, Your Honor. I'm filing this amended witness list," said Brent, handing a copy to Stein and Black.

"Your Honor, this is unfair surprise! We were never advised of this witness before," said Stein.

"Mr. Marks says he's an impeachment witness. To impeach whom, Mr. Marks?"

"The testimony of Mr. Bernstein, Your Honor. I'm just laying the foundation for it."

"And you intend to call this witness next?"

"Yes, Your Honor. I have him on subpoena. He's in custody, right next door in the holding cell."

"Then proceed, Mr. Marks, but, since this is only foundational, keep it short."

"Mr. Bernstein, do you know a Kevin Suskind?"

"I need to talk to my lawyer."

"Move to strike as non-responsive."

"Granted. You will answer the question, Mr. Bernstein."

"I need to talk to my lawyer."

"Your Honor, please instruct the witness to answer the question."

"Your Honor," said Black, I would like a word with my client.

"Mr. Black, your client has been testifying all morning. If he needs your counsel, he can have it on the breaks. Now, Mr. Bernstein, please answer the question. Do you know a Kevin Suskind?"

"I refuse to answer that question on Fifth Amendment grounds," said Bernstein.

The collective sigh of shock came like a wave over the courtroom.

"Your Honor, my client claims his privilege against self-incrimination and will not answer any further questions," said Black.

"Your Honor, Mr. Bernstein has waived his privilege against self-incrimination," argued Brent. The argument did not go far at the bench. Bernstein would not be testifying anymore, and Brent wouldn't get a peep out of Suskind, but the implication to the jury was clear – Bernstein was guilty.

At the bench, Stein and Black made an unusual request. "Your Honor, in light of this development, the defense requests a recess," said Stein.

"And the purpose of that recess?"

"To discuss settlement with my client."

"Very well, Mr. Stein, we will queue up the next witness for the plaintiff, but all of the time you use will be coming out of your trial time if there turns out to be no settlement."

"Understood, Your Honor."

"Ladies and gentlemen of the jury, the defendant has refused to further testify on the grounds that it may incriminate him. He has a constitutional privilege not to further testify and you may not infer from his exercise of the privilege or his silence that he is guilty of any crime or use it as proof of any issue in this proceeding," said Masters.

Jack London said, "Life is not always a matter of holding good cards, but playing a poor hand well." Brent was likely holding a losing hand, but he had a hell of a bluff going.

54

Brent used the time to prepare April, in the small cafeteria of the courthouse. Since her assessment of the case and Brent's were, most likely, drastically different, even if they were to get an excellent offer, she could reject it, the case would go to the jury, and Brent was not confident that they had presented enough evidence to win. Not only that, the potentially deadly threat of "Mike the Cleaner" still lingered in his mind.

"Can you explain to me what's going on?" she asked.

"Kevin Suskind was just arrested, after a high speed chase and a shootout with the police, where he shot an FBI agent."

"Oh my God! Who is he?"

"Agent Wollard matched a hair sample taken from Suskind to one found at your parent's house."

April started to cry. "So he's the one who murdered my parents. And Bernstein doesn't want to testify because he's in on it. I knew it!"

"Now, don't go so fast."

"Are they going to prosecute him for the murder?"

"It's too soon to tell. Right now, Suskind has been arrested in connection with Rick Penn's disappearance."

"Then this is good for us, isn't it? I mean, good for the case."

"Yes and no."

"What do you mean 'yes and no'?"

"Yes, it points to Bernstein's guilt, but no, I don't think it's enough to establish the predicate act for RICO."

"The jury heard him."

"And they were instructed to ignore it."

"But they heard it."

"Yes, they heard it, but that doesn't mean that they'll vote in our favor. We have to establish that predicate act, and you know it's always been the weakest link of our case."

"What are you saying?"

"I'm saying that their offer before was to walk away from the home loan. Now I think they will come back with some serious money. They can't afford to have this get out in the press, win or lose."

"Well good then, let's go for it!"

"And if we lose?"

"Then we lose."

"April, you've lost your mother, and your father. This is a chance to punish the bank and make them pay. The money won't bring them back, or ease your pain, but you will be able to keep their house, mortgage free, and have some money to give to their future grandchildren. I'm sure they would have wanted this for you."

"Do what you need to do Brent, but you know my answer."

55

Charles Stinson used to say that "a good compromise is one where both parties walk away disappointed." He also said, "Whoever gives the first number loses." That phrase stuck in Brent's mind when a smiling Joe Stein approached him, swinging his briefcase.

"Counselor, let's talk turkey," Stein said.

"We're on your dime, talk away."

"My client realizes that your client has suffered great losses. Of course, in my estimation, they could never be held responsible for these losses."

"Of course."

"But, nevertheless, Bernstein's taking the Fifth is a fuck up. I don't think you have enough evidence to win this case, but it's worth it to the bank to cover your client's fees and incidental costs, if we can get a confidential settlement."

"It would take a lot more than incidental costs to settle this case," said Brent.

"You've discussed it with your client. How much will it take to settle the case?"

Smiling slyly, Brent said, "You tell me. You're the one who asked for the time away from the trial to talk settlement. You can't be coming to me just now after the past hour just to get to a starting point."

"Fair enough."

"Somebody's got to give a number, Joe, and it's not going to be me. My client wants this case to go to the jury, win or lose."

"That's not a very wise decision."

"So we're at a Mexican standoff? Let's go back to the courtroom." Brent starting walking toward the courtroom like a tourist bargaining for a sombrero in Tijuana.

"Wait."

Brent stopped, but paused before turning, so as not to appear too anxious.

"Yes?"

"Quiet title to the house, plus $1 million in costs, that's our final offer."

Smiling from the inside, because he realized that Stein had already lost the upper hand of negotiation, but with a stern look of disappointment on his face, Brent said, "Joe, like you said, I've talked with my client. This is not going to cut it. You've got to go back to the bank because I know she's going to reject it. But I've got an obligation to communicate it to her, so I will."

***

"A million? Forget it!" said April, defiantly.

"I knew you would say that," said Brent.

"These are my parents, Brent, I can't put a price on them. Three hundred million would not be enough."

"You can't ever get them back either."

"I know," April sobbed. "This whole case has been a disaster, and I feel like those bastards are winning and just laughing at us."

"April, you came to the court for justice. Unfortunately, you're not going to find it here. I feel very strongly that we're likely to lose on the RICO count. You're basically asking the jury to convict Prudent Bank of not only bank fraud, but murder."

"Bernstein killed her."

"That may be true, but that doesn't mean the bank is responsible. If he did it, as opposed to doing them a favor, he probably created even more of a mess for them."

"I just don't see how I can reduce my parents' lives to dollars and cents."

"You can't. Nobody who sues because they lost a child, or a wife or husband, or anyone close to them can ever be compensated for that loss with money. But it's the only way the law has to force the guilty party to make amends."

"What about the death penalty, or life in prison?"

"April, you know this is not a criminal case. But, after Bernstein took the Fifth, I wouldn't be surprised if a criminal prosecution is around the corner."

"I could use the money to establish a fund in their name to help victims of bank fraud."

"That's an idea."

"Now I just need to get your bottom line. What's the least amount of money, plus my fees, plus the house, that will settle this case? I won't tell them that; I just need that number to negotiate."

April thought long and hard. "I wouldn't settle for less than $3 million," she finally said.

Now April had lost her advantage in the negotiation, because Brent had her number. It would not bring George Marsh or Rick Penn back, but it would keep Brent and April from joining them, and it would be a victory as well as an end to the case which had taken so much away from both of them.

"I'll see what I can do," he said.

56

A stern and impatient looking Virginia Masters took the bench, outside the jury's presence.

"In the matter of Marsh v. Prudent Bank, we are outside the presence of the jury. What is happening gentlemen, do we have a settlement or not?"

"We're working on it, Your Honor," said Stein.

"Well, that's not good enough, Mr. Stein. You have half an hour more. I suggest you call your client and do your best to settle this case if that's what you want to do because in half an hour, I expect to see the jury in the box and the next witness in that chair."

"Yes, Your Honor."

*　*　*

"You've gotta do better than $1 million, Joe," said Brent, in the corridor outside the courtroom.

"Look, Brent, just give me your client's number. I'll take it to mine and see if we can get this done."

"I don't have a number."

"You don't know what your client will take?"

"I know what she won't take."

"Look kid, don't bullshit me. I'm a bigger bullshitter than you, and I can smell it a mile away."

"My client's not hearing anything that would compel her not to go forward. We've already put on our case."

"Which sucks."

"Your opinion. If you think the jury shares that opinion, fair enough. But I don't think either one of us has a crystal ball."

"Alright. We've got less than 20 minutes now. Let me make a phone call."

"Do what you have to do."

***

It took Stein no more than five minutes to come back, which told Brent that he already had his bottom line; the maximum amount that he had authority to settle for. Brent knew the minimum his client would go for. Now it was just a matter of who cracked first.

"1.5 and not a penny more."

"Sorry, that won't do it."

"For Christ's sake man, what does she want?"

"Justice."

"You know what I mean."

"Joe, if I take that figure to my client, we're done. She won't take it, period. So if it's your bottom line, let's get on with the trial." Brent turned to walk away again.

"Don't walk away from me. I know that's a bullshit move."

Brent turned, smiling. "Let's go Joe, our time's almost up."

"Two million."

"Four."

"Are you crazy?"

"Four million, Joe, that's our bottom line."

"Let me make a phone call."

Stein came back faster than the last time. "Three and not a penny more." Hearing the magic words, Brent said, "We have a deal." Stein looked relieved.

57

Judge Masters thanked the jury for their service, and excused them, and took the settlement on the record. April, relieved that she had some kind of closure, thanked Brent, and left the courtroom. That left Brent alone with Stein.

"Are you going to talk to the jury?" he asked. After a trial is over, the admonition of not talking about the case is lifted and lawyers always have a chance to talk to the jury if they want.

"No."

"Why not?"

"I don't want to know," said Brent. "What I do want to know is how close I got to your bottom line."

"It was $5 million. Never bullshit a bullshitter, son."

Brent felt instantly deflated. Up until then, he thought he had made the best deal he could make for his client.

"Don't be disappointed. You fought a good fight," said Stein, slapping Brent on the shoulder. Brent shook Stein's hand.

"See you around, Joe."

"Better hope you don't," said Stein, laughing, as he packed up his briefcase.

58

Kevin Suskind trudged to the mess hall with his group to have his first taste of jail food. He needed to get out; needed to get high more than anything else. The meeting with his lawyer had gone well. He had the best legal defense that money could buy. And once his bail was posted, he would be out of this shit hole. The food was crappy, but he was famished, so he ate well.

As Suskind shuffled back to his cell block, he stopped to watch two inmates going at it.

"What the fuck you lookin' at?" said the fat one.

"You, lard ass!" said the skinny one.

Suskind laughed. *What a couple of idiots.*

"Keep moving," said the Deputy, about the time that the two unlikely warriors went at it, brawling. The Deputy's attention was called to the fight, and radioed it in, as two other deputies descended on the fighters to break them up.

Suskind felt a pain under his chin as a warm slush of blood covered his jump suit from the red fountain flowing from his carotid artery. He covered the wound with his hand, but it was no use. The heart pumps blood at five liters per minute. Suskind fell to his knees as the crowd around him disbursed and two deputies came to his aid, but it was too late.

59

William Conlan got behind the wheel of his BMW Z4 and floored it. The one thing he loved most in life was speed. Whether it was flying down the road at 90 miles per hour or doing the same flying in his head, fast was the only way to go.

The long drive to San Francisco on Highway One was treacherous, but that's what made it so much fun. Many people traveled this road for the beautiful coastline. Conlan did it for the thrills. Every twisting turn was a new rush of adrenaline; especially when you tweaked it with his drug of choice – crystal methamphetamine; the poor man's cocaine. His buddy Kevin Suskind had an expensive cocaine habit. Crystal meth gave Conlan the same bump, and saved him money for fast cars and fast women.

Conlan jumped over the solid double yellow line, passing every car at will. Every curve was an exhilarating rush. The fog hovered over the hills of the coast, peppered with pines. Conlan passed a bunch on motorcycles like they were standing still; provoking a memory of the bar fight at the Cold Spring Tavern.

The fog burned away to a powder blue sky as Conlan pushed the Z4 to its limits, but felt himself losing control going into the hairpin curve. He pushed the brakes gently to correct the shift, but the lifeless brake pedal just hit the floor. Panicked, Conlan hit the brake pedal again, then tried to gear down, but the momentum propelled the Z4 through the metal guard rail and over the cliff. That flight was the last fulfillment of Conlan's need for speed.

* * *

Mike the cleaner answered his cell phone, as he munched on an In-N-Out Double Double in his car. His cell phone rang, a business call.

"Good. One more to go. Let me know." Mike clicked off the cell phone and kept munching on the burger.

60

When he went to bed that night, Steven Bernstein was worried. He was worried about being arrested. But he was more worried about the literally bloody mess he had made for his employer, and that, as a result, he may not have a job the next day. He was so worried about it, in fact, he took a Halcion so he could sleep. Bernstein had stayed up late, writing a letter of regret to his employer, apologizing for having put the company through so much grief. He worked on the note until he became drowsy. *No matter,* he thought. *I'll finish it in the morning.* Finally, the Halcion took effect and he was able to drift off.

Bernstein had a nightmare that night. He dreamed he saw a ghost at the foot of his bed. It was one of those terrifying dreams; the kind where your body surges with adrenaline, urging you to act, but, because you are asleep, you cannot move. He tried to scream, but the voice would not come. He tried to jump out of the bed and run as the ghost approached, but was immobilized; unable to move any of his muscles. The ghost came closer to his side, then disappeared. *Thank God it was only a dream,* he thought.

* * *

Two days later, Bernstein's body was found by his housekeeper. On his nightstand was an empty bottle of Halcion and an unfinished suicide note.

EPILOGUE

It was all too clean, all too neat. April was right. The bank had gotten away with murder. But not the murder of her parents. That was, most likely, the work of Bernstein and his "kill for hire" team. Now those silent truths were buried forever.

Brent pondered it as he looked out at the harbor. It was a crystal clear day, and the horizon was a thin, defined line between cobalt and sky blue. The air was as fresh as the ocean spray. The fishing boats were running, the whale watcher boats were filled with tourists looking for packs of dolphins and humpbacks. The world seemed normal again, but it would never be the same.

So much had been lost in this case. April's parents, Brent's best friend, and almost Angela. And, in the end, the bank just got out its checkbook and it all went away. He remembered Joshua Banks, who always spoke in bible verses and the one that seemed appropriate now was the love of money. It certainly was the root of all evil.

The world could not be changed with one court case. *It might take another,* thought Brent.

AFTERWORD

Of course, this story is fictional, but it is based on solid historical research. If you care to read on, I have summarized some of the research. If not, I would like to ask you now to please leave a review on Amazon. Finally, I love to get email from my readers. Please feel free to send me one at info@kennetheade.com. I would also like you to join my mailing list, for advance notice of new books, free excerpts, free books and updates. I will never spam you. Please subscribe here: http://bit.do/mailing-list.

The financial meltdown of 2008 was not the result of mysterious economic forces. What caused it was rampant fraud in the financial markets. Before the 2008 mortgage crisis, thousands of subprime real estate loans on over-appraised real estate were assigned to mortgage pools and then resold to investors as mortgage backed securities. When U.S. home prices declined sharply after peaking in 2006, it became difficult for borrowers to refinance those loans. As adjustable rate mortgages began to increase in monthly payments, mortgage delinquencies soared, causing mortgage backed securities to lose most of their value. This, in turn, led to what is known as the financial crisis of 2008 – the worst financial crisis since the Great Depression.

The big banks were on the verge of failure. Instead of letting them fail, the Government enacted the "Emergency Economic Stabilization Act of 2008" and bailed them out. The Act authorized the U.S. Treasury to spend up to $700 billion to purchase devalued and virtually worthless bank assets, especially mortgage backed securities, which provided billions of dollars in cash to the banks. Unfortunately, programs to help consumers avoid foreclosures did not get as much support as the bank bailout. They only got lip service.

Bank fraud played the major role in the crisis, by deceiving investors who purchased mortgage backed securities. But holding the banks responsible for the disaster could have plunged them back into insolvency all over again, so the biggest banks have paid relatively small fines in relation to the profits that they have reaped from the bailout and recovery of assets. In short, not only did they get away with murder, but, thanks to the bailout, their profits are at an all time high. And, with a few notable exceptions, bank executives who took part in the fraud were able to keep their huge bonuses, escape criminal and civil liability, and fly away on their golden parachutes.

One more thing...

I hope you have enjoyed this book and I am thankful that you have spent the time to get to this point, which means that you must have received something from reading it. If you turn to the last page, Kindle will give you the opportunity to rate the book and share your thoughts through an automatic feed to your Facebook and Twitter accounts. If you believe your friends would enjoy this book, I would be honored if you would post your thoughts, and also leave a review on Amazon. Please click here to leave your review.

Best regards,

Kenneth Eade

info@kennetheade.com

BONUS OFFER

Sign up for paperback discounts, free stuff, advance sale notifications of this and other books by clicking here: http://bit.do/mailing-list. I promise I will never spam you.

ABOUT THE AUTHOR

Author Kenneth Eade, best known for his legal and political thrillers, practiced law for 30 years before publishing his first novel, "An Involuntary Spy." Eade, an up-and-coming author in the legal thriller and courtroom drama genre, has been described by critics as "one of our strongest thriller writers on the scene, and the fact that he draws his stories from the contemporary philosophical landscape is very much to his credit." Critics have also said that "his novels will remind readers of John Grisham, proving that Kenneth Eade deserves to be on the same lists with the world's greatest thriller authors."

Says Eade of the comparisons: "John Grisham is famous for saying that sometimes he likes to wrap a good story around an important issue. In all of my novels, the story and the important issues are always present."

Eade is known to keep in touch with his readers, offering free gifts and discounts to all those who sign up at his web site, www.kennetheade.com.

.

Made in the USA
Middletown, DE
05 October 2016